DARRY THE LIFE SAVER; OR, THE HEROES OF THE COAST

BY

Frank V. Webster

DARRY THE LIFE SAVER; OR, THE HEROES OF THE COAST

Published by Epic House Publishers

New York City, NY

First published circa 1995

Copyright © Epic House Publishers, 2015

All rights reserved

ABOUT EPIC HOUSE PUBLISHERS

Few things get the adrenaline going like fast-paced action, and with that in mind, **Epic House Publishers** can give readers the world's best action and adventure novels and stories in the click of a button, whether it's Tarzan on land or Moby Dick in the sea.

DARRY, THE LIFE SAVER: CHAPTER I: THE HURRICANE

"Will we ever weather this terrible storm?"

It was a half-grown lad who flung this despairing question out; the wind carried the sound of his voice off over the billows; but there came no answer.

A brigantine, battered by the tropical hurricane sweeping up from the Caribbean Sea, was staggering along like a wounded beast. Her masts had long since gone by the board, and upon the stump of the mizzen-stick a bit of canvas like a goose-wing had been spread in the useless endeavor to maintain steerageway.

All around, the sea rose and fell in mountainous waves, on which the poor wreck tossed about, as helpless as a cork.

Though the lad, lashed to some of the rigging that still clung to the temporary jury mast, strained his eyes to the utmost, he could see nothing but the waste of waves, the uplifting tops of which curled over, and were snatched away in flying spud by the furious wind.

Darry was the cabin boy of the Falcon, having sailed with Captain Harley now for several years. The old navigator had run across him in a foreign port, and under most peculiar conditions.

Hearing a boyish voice that somehow struck his fancy, raised in angry protest, followed by the crack of a whip, and much loud laughing, the skipper of the brigantine had pushed into a café in Naples.

Here he discovered a small, but sturdy lad, who had apparently been playing a violin for coppers, refusing to dance for a big brute of a sailor, an Italian, who had seized upon his beloved instrument.

When the boy had made an effort to recover the violin the bully deliberately smashed it on the back of a chair.

Then, laughing at the poor little chap's expressions of grief as he gathered up the pieces tenderly in his arms, the brutal sailor had seized upon a carter's whip, and cracking it loudly, declared that he would lay it over the boy's shoulders unless he mounted a table and danced to his whistling.

It was then that the big mariner strode in and stood between the lad and his cowardly persecutors.

When good-hearted Captain Harley heard the boy's pitiful story, and that he was a waif, having been abandoned some years before by an old man with whom he seemed to have been traveling, he offered to befriend him, and give him a chance to see something of the world as cabin boy on the good old brigantine, Falcon.

This offer the little chap had eagerly accepted, for he believed he must be of American birth, and somehow longed to set foot on that land far across the sea.

Some years had passed.

Darry knew no other home save the friendly cabin of the brigantine, and since he had no knowledge as to what his name might be, by degrees he came to assume that of his benefactor.

During these years the boy had seen much of the world, and learned many things under the guidance of the warm-hearted captain.

Of course he spent many bitter hours in vain regrets over the fact that there was so little chance of his ever learning his identity—only a slender link seemed to connect him with that mysterious past that was hidden from his sight; and this was a curious little scar upon his right arm just below the elbow.

It looked like a crescent moon, and had been there ever since he could remember.

This fact caused Darry to believe it might be the result of some accident that must have occurred while he was yet a baby.

If such were the case then some people, somewhere, would be apt to recognize this peculiar mark if they ever saw it again.

Captain Harley had always encouraged him in the belief that some happy day he would surely know the truth.

Just now, however, it really looked as though Darry need no longer allow himself to feel any anxiety on that score.

The ocean depths would offer just as easy a resting place to a nameless waif as to a crowned monarch.

When the great waves broke over the drifting vessel the rush of water must have swept him away, only that he had been wise enough to lash himself to the stump of the mizzen-mast.

During a little lull in the tempest someone joined him, also using the whipping rope-ends to secure his hold.

Darry saw by the aid of the darting lightning that it was his good friend, the captain; and with his thoughts still taken up with the peril of his situation he repeated the question that only the mocking winds had heard before:

"Will we ever weather this storm, captain?"

"I fear not, my lad," replied the master of the ship, sadly, "the poor old hulk is now only a plaything for the elements. It looks as though the Falcon had reached the end of her voyaging at last. Twenty years have I commanded her. I have a feeling that if so be she goes down I will not survive her."

The roar of the gale was such that it became necessary to shout at times, in order to make one's self heard above the elements.

"Are we near the coast?" asked the boy, anxiously; for he knew that such a thing must double their danger.

"I am afraid it is only too true, though the storm has been so prolonged that I have long ago lost my reckoning," replied the mariner.

"But you told me these coasts are patrolled by brave life savers, who always stand ready to risk everything in case a vessel is driven on the reefs?" continued the boy, trying to see a gleam of hope through the gloom.

"That is true, but alas! I am afraid even the bravest of men would find themselves helpless in such a terrific blow as this."

"But, captain, surely you have not given up all hope?" anxiously demanded Darry, trying to face the terrible prospect with a brave heart.

"I never do that, lad. But one of us may not live to reach the shore; and since it is so, I wanted to have a few last words with you, and then I must return to my duty, which is to try and steer this drifting hulk until the end comes."

He reached out his hand.

The boy eagerly clutched it, and there, as the lightning flashed, he looked into the kind face of his benefactor.

Something seemed to tell him that it was the last time he would ever feel the pressure of that friendly hand, and this thought alarmed him as the storm had thus far been unable to do.

"Listen, and take heed, my lad," said the skipper, earnestly, "it may be that Providence will shield you through this time of trouble, and that you shall reach the shore in safety after all. Should ill befall me I want you to write my old mother up in York State—you know where she lives. I have made all preparations, so that she will be provided for, and my sister also. Do you understand me?"

"Oh! yes, sir! But I hope we may both pull through!" cried the boy, earnestly.

"So do I, for life is sweet; but it may not be. Now, lad, about yourself, and I am done. Remember all that I have taught you. Then you will grow up to be a true man. And continue to search for some evidence of your people. That mark on your arm may be of great value to you some day. Hark! I fancied I caught the sound of the breakers just then! It is possible that the time has come for us to part. Good bye, my boy, and God bless you whatever betide!"

Another fierce pressure of the hand, and Captain Harley was gone.

Standing there, filled with horror and dismay, Darry caught a last glimpse of his guardian staggering across the wet deck, and then the gloom forever hid him from view.

The days would come, and the days would go, but always must he remember that the last thought of the noble captain was for him.

He strained his hearing to ascertain whether the captain's fears were well founded, and it was not long before he too could catch the awful pounding of the seas upon the half-submerged reefs.

The helpless brigantine was drifting slowly, but surely to her fate; for there was hardly a place along the whole American coast more dangerous than this, which had in times past proved a graveyard for many noble ships.

Among the tangled rigging was a broken spar, and to this Darry lashed himself, in the faint hope that if it were swept ashore he might still cling to life.

He awaited the impending crash with his heart cold within his breast; for after all he was but a lad, and the strongest men might have viewed the catastrophe with a sickening sense of dread.

Then came a fearful shock, as the brigantine was smashed down upon the jaws of the reef by a mighty force.

After that the seas had her for a plaything, rushing completely over her as if in derision.

Three times the boy was almost drowned by the flood that poured across that slanting deck, and he knew that if he remained there longer his time had surely come. It would be better to cut loose from the mast, and trust his fortunes upon the breast of the next giant wave that, if it were kind, would carry him well over the rocks, and head him for the distant beach.

It was in sheer desperation that he seized upon his sailor's knife and severed the ropes that thus far had held so securely.

Then he awaited the coming of the next comber with set teeth, and held his breath.

A few seconds and it was upon him.

This time the spar, as well as the clinging lad, went sweeping over the side of the vessel, and carried safely above the reef, started in toward the beach on a roller that seemed gigantic.

The spray was in his eyes, so that he could hardly see at all, but at that moment Darry thought he glimpsed a light somewhere ahead; and what the captain had told him about the gallant life savers flashed into his mind.

Somehow, it seemed to give the despairing boy renewed hope.

Perhaps these brave men were watching for the coming of just such flotsam from the wreck, which they must have sighted when the lightning flashed; and would find some means for plucking him out of the raging sea.

CHAPTER II: SAVED BY THE LIFE CHAIN

The line of reefs stood as a barrier to the sea, and after the waves came in contact with the rocks they continued on their course with less violence than before.

Still, it was terrible enough to any one exposed to their fury.

Hope soars high in the breast of youth, however, and life is sweet, so that our hero continued to struggle against the forces to which he found himself exposed.

Again had his eyes caught a glimpse of a burning light on the shore, and somehow it gave him renewed courage to hold on, for he seemed to understand that determined hearts were waiting there, eager to give him a helping hand.

Then some object sped past him, and he caught the sight of flashing oars.

It was the lifeboat!

In spite of the great danger involved in the undertaking, the coast guards had succeeded in launching their boat, and were even now heading toward the wreck on the reef; though the chances of finding a single living soul aboard seemed small indeed, for the billows were breaking completely over her, and she must soon go to pieces.

Darry tried to call out, but his mouth filled with salty water, and in despair he saw the boat pass him by.

Even the lightning failed to illumine the scene just then, or some eager eye might have detected the floating spar and its human burden.

No hope remained save that he might be tossed up on the beach somewhere near the friendly fire that was burning as a beacon.

Once he fancied he heard men shouting during a lull in the roar of the elements; but the coming of another smothering billow shut out the friendly sounds.

Closer he was flung, until he could again hear the shouts of men, but the baffling seas kept playing with him, sending him up on the breaking wave only to once more snatch him back, until the poor boy almost despaired of living through the dreadful ordeal.

He tried his best to raise his voice, but the cry he gave utterance to was so feeble that even if heard it must have been taken for the note of some storm bird attracted by the light of the beacon fire.

Just when he was giving way to despair, he saw the figures of men running along the beach close to the edge of the waves, and new hope awoke in his breast that his predicament had been seen.

Now they were pushing into the sea, holding one another's hands, and forming a living chain, with a sturdy fellow at the end to snatch the victim of the wreck out of the jaws of death.

The precious sight was at that instant shut out, for again there came a deluge of water from behind, overwhelming the boy on the floating spar.

Darry felt something take hold upon him, which, in his excited condition, he at first believed to be a shark; but, on the contrary, it proved to be the fingers of the man at the outer end of the line.

Once they closed upon the person of the shipwrecked cabin boy they could not be easily induced to let go, and amid shouts of triumph, spar and lad were speedily dragged up on the beach beyond reach of the hungry waves.

He was dimly conscious of being released from his friendly float, and tenderly carried a short distance to the shelter of a house.

It was the life-saving station to which the boy had been taken by his rescuers.

HE WAS DIMLY CONSCIOUS OF BEING RELEASED FROM HIS FRIENDLY FLOAT.

Here he was wrapped in blankets, and placed close to a warm fire in order to restore his benumbed faculties; while some hot liquid being forced between his pallid lips served to give new strength to his body.

In less than ten minutes he opened his eyes and looked around.

Kind faces, even though rough and bearded, surrounded him, and he knew that for once he had cheated the sea of a victim.

As strength came back he began to take an interest in what was passing around him, especially when he saw several men carried in, whom he recognized as some of the sailors of the ill-fated brigantine.

Eagerly he watched and prayed that his good friend the captain might be one of those who had been snatched from a watery grave; but as time passed this hope gradually became fainter.

The lifeboat had managed to return from the wreck, to report that not a living soul remained aboard; and that the seas were so tremendous that even had it been otherwise there would have been small chance of saving them, since it was next to impossible to approach close to the vessel.

How the boy, lying there, looked with almost reverence upon those stalwart fellows who were risking their lives in the effort to save their fellow men.

Darry would never forget that hour.

The impressions he received then would remain with him through life; and in his eyes the calling of a life saver must always be reckoned the noblest vocation to which a young man could pledge himself.

He thought he would like nothing better than to become one of the band, and in some way repay the great debt he owed them by doing as he had been done by.

Presently he had so far recovered that he could get up and move around.

All of the sailors had not been equally fortunate; indeed, two of them would never again scour the seas, having taken out papers for that long voyage the end of which no mortal eye can see.

As each new arrival was carried in the boy would be the first to hasten forward, but as often his sigh echoed the heavy feeling in his heart as he discovered a face other than the familiar one he had grown to love.

One of the surfmen who had manned the lifeboat seemed to be particularly interested in the rescued boy, for he came into the station several times to ask how he was feeling, and if there was not something more he wanted.

He was a tall, angular fellow, with a thin but engaging face, and Darry had heard some of the others call him Abner Peake.

Somehow he found himself drawn toward this man from the start; and it seemed as though in losing one good friend he had found another to take the place of the kind captain.

Abner was a native of the shore, and spoke in the peculiar dialect of the uneducated Southerner; but as a water-dog he knew no superior, and it is this quality that Uncle Sam looks for when making up his crews to man the life-saving stations that dot the whole coast from Maine to Florida.

There was a twang about his voice that reminded Darry of a negro he had once had for a shipmate on the brigantine; but at the same time his tone was soft, and inspired confidence.

"Better hev a leetle more coffee, bub?" he said, coming upon Darry as the latter turned away white-faced from the last body carried in by the rough men.

"Perhaps it would do me good; I still feel mighty weak; but I'm glad to be here instead of out there," replied Darry, pointing to where the white-capped waves were rushing in long lines toward the beach.

"Course yuh be, bub. And we-uns air glad tuh get a chanct tuh pull yuh outen the water. My old woman'd like tuh set eyes on yuh. Jest the age our Joe would a-ben if he'd pulled through," and the rough surfman swept his sleeve across his eyes as he spoke.

The secret of his interest in Darry was out; he had lost a boy of his own, and his heart was very tender still, so that the sight of this poor shipwrecked lad brought back his own sorrow keenly.

"You haven't seen anything of the captain, I suppose?" anxiously asked Darry, wondering if it could possibly be that he had missed sight of his friend at the time he was lying there unconscious.

Abner Peake shook his head in the negative.

He saw the boy was very eager to learn of the mariner's fate, and well he knew that with each passing minute the chances of the other surviving the pounding of the seas became less and less.

It was now not far from dawn.

The hurricane still blew with its old violence, and there was scant hope of its passing for another twelve hours at least.

All that time those devoted men must be on the watch, ready to man their surfboat again and take their lives in hand, should another vessel strike the dangerous reefs that were marked upon the chart as the worst within a hundred miles of Hatteras.

Sick at heart over the loss of his wise friend and benefactor, Darry found the interior of the station almost unbearable just then.

He felt as though he must get outside where the elements rioted, and watch the incoming waves for some sign of the captain.

But this new-found friend declared that it could do no good, since the beach was already patrolled by those whose keen eyes would discover the faintest trace of a brave swimmer trying to buffet the cruel waves; he must remain under cover, so as to escape the possible evil results of his late experience.

And so Darry had to once more lie down and let the other cover him with a blanket, a pillow having been placed under his head.

He was utterly exhausted, and it had only been hope and excitement that had buoyed him up until now.

As he lay there watching the various things that were being done for the relief of the poor fellows snatched from a watery grave he found his eyes growing heavy, and occasionally closing in spite of his efforts to remain awake.

Once he sat up as some men came in bearing another sailor who, alas, had apparently been dragged out of the sea too late to save the spark of life; but, upon learning that it was not the one in whose fate he was so keenly interested, Darry had fallen back again upon his hard pillow.

Soon after things faded from his sight, and he slept the sleep of weariness, for every muscle in his body was as sore as though it had been pounded with a club.

It was hours before he awoke.

At first he could not understand just where he was or how he came in such unfamiliar surroundings; but seeing the kindly face of Abner Peake bending over, he asked a mute question that the other answered with a shake of his head.

The captain's body had not as yet come ashore.

CHAPTER III: ABNER PEAKE'S OFFER

Days passed. Darry had entirely given up hope of ever hearing from the captain, whose body must have been carried out to sea again, as were several of the crew.

After the shock became less severe, our hero began to take a new interest in the scene around him, and particularly in connection with the life-saving station where his new friend Abner was quartered.

The keeper was a grizzled surfman named Frazer, and a man possessed of some education; he did not awaken the same feelings in the boy as Abner Peake, but at the same time he was evidently inclined to be friendly in his own gruff way.

On the third day after the rescue he called Darry to him as he sat mending a net with which the crew of the station secured enough fish to serve them for an occasional meal.

"Sit down, lad. I want to talk with you a bit," he said.

Darry dropped on a block close by.

He was still filled with the deepest admiration for these men of the coast, and his determination to follow their arduous calling when he grew big enough to take an oar in the surfboat was undiminished.

"Now, tell me about yourself, and where you belong. We are not allowed to keep any rescued sailors more than a certain time. You notice that all the others have gone, save the poor chaps lying under those mounds yonder. Being a boy you've been favored; but the time has come to know what you mean to do. Speak up, lad, and tell me your story?"

Encouraged by his kind voice, Darry told all he knew about himself up to the very moment when he parted from his friend, the captain.

Mr. Frazer seemed interested.

"I feel sorry for you, Darry. It must be hard to feel that you haven't got a friend in the world. My hands are tied in the matter, so I can do nothing; but there's Abner Peake telling me he'd like you to stay with him," he remarked.

"I understood him to say he once had a boy about my age."

"Yes, a likely little chap, but it was about a year back he was lost."

"Was he drowned?" asked Darry, feeling that this was about the way most persons in this coast country must meet their end.

"Yes. The little fellow was a venturesome boy, and tried to cross the bay in a heavy sea. He must have been swept out at the inlet. They found the boat on the beach, three miles above here, but never little Joe. Abner has never gotten over it. To this day he sits and looks out to sea as if he could discover his poor boy coming back to him. I thought for a time the fellow would go out of his mind."

"And he wants me to stay with him?" continued Darry, musingly.

"Yes. Abner has a small house out of the village, where his wife and the two little girls live, while he is over here at the station. Often we want someone to cross over with supplies, and he thinks you might like the job."

Darry drew a long breath.

"I have no home. The only one I ever knew was the poor old Falcon, and her timbers are scattered along the coast for ten miles. I think that if Mr. Peake really wants me to stay with him I shall accept gladly. It is tough to feel like a piece of driftwood all the time," he said.

"I think you are wise in deciding that way. Abner is a kind man, and as for his wife—well, she's got a temper all right, but if you don't rub it the wrong way she can be got on with, I reckon. Anyhow, it would pay you to try it until something else turns up. Maybe you want to ship on another vessel?"

"I think I have had all of the sea I want, after that time. I wake up nights, thinking I'm choking with the salt water, and trying to catch my breath. When I get older and stronger I want to be a life saver like you, sir."

The keeper smiled pleasantly.

It was not often he appeared as a hero in the eyes of even a boy, and, being human, he could not help feeling some satisfaction.

"It's a dangerous calling, Darry; but, after all, no worse than that of a sailor. And while we risk our lives often, it is to try and save others. There's some satisfaction in that. But there sits Abner on that old keel of a wreck; suppose you go and tell him your story, and see what he says."

When the boy joined him Abner Peake looked up, and the solemn expression on his face changed to one of kindliness.

"Set down, lad. Are yuh feelin' all right agin after your rough time?" he asked.

"A little sore in the arms still, but that will pass away soon. Mr. Frazer told me you wanted to hear my story."

"If yuh don't mind tellin' me. I reckoned as how yuh must 'a' had a hard time. Now, I ain't never been away from this here coast, but I feels for boys what's out in the wide world. Still, there's some hope o' them comin' back tuh the nest agin, some day. Now, go on, lad," with a long-drawn sigh.

Again did the homeless Darry start in to narrate his brief career, so far as it was known to him; and the old surfman listened with a tear in his eye, as he told of his abandonment in a foreign port, and the hard time he had getting enough to eat.

Finally it was all told, and Abner Peake laid a hand on his arm, saying:

"Don't say yuh ain't got a home, any more, Darry, if so be yuh'd care to stay at my place. The missus ain't the easiest one in the world tuh get along with, but soon as she sees what a likely chap yuh be I know she'll like yuh, same as I do. Try it awhile, lad, until yuh kin make your mind up. My Joe used tuh make a tidy lot of money trappin' animals in the swamp for ther skins, huntin' turkles like them terrapin they pay sech a big price fur, an' actin' as guide fur the shooters as come down along the coast after ducks and snipe and bay birds. No reason but what you could do the same. Only try and git on the good side of the ole woman, to begin with, lad. She's got a heart, tho' there's some as don't believe it. I know she's still a feelin' bad because Joe was taken from us."

"It was hard to lose him, your only boy," said Darry, consolingly.

The man shook his head dolefully, and bent a wistful look toward the open sea.

"Yes, it was tough; but I reckon he's safe in the harbor long afore now. What say, lad, be yuh of a mind to try it with us?" he continued eagerly.

"I will, and only glad of the chance. It is kind of you to make me the offer, and I only hope I may be able to please your wife. I'll do everything I can to take the place of Joe, although, of course, I couldn't expect to do that altogether," replied Darry.

"Say, yuh make me feel better, already. Seems to me as if I heerd little Joe aspeakin' to me from somewhere. I'm goin' crost the bay to-night, lad. It's my turn for a day off, an' I'll take yuh with me. I reckons his clothes'd just about be the right fit fur yuh."

So it was settled.

Darry felt easy in his mind now, much more so than he had been ever since finding himself adrift on shore, like a vessel without an anchor.

No matter how humble, it would be home to him, for he had no memories to haunt him, and bring about discontent.

There was the village near by, where possibly he might meet boys of his own age; and what Abner had said about the pursuits by which Joe had been accustomed to making odd bits of money appealed to him, for he believed he had something of a love for outdoor sports in his nature, since he had never neglected to take advantage of a chance to use a fishing line, when the brigantine happened to be in one of the world ports to which business called her.

But above all he gloried in the fact that occasionally he would have the opportunity to visit the station on the outer beach, where those hardy men patrolled every night, and stood ready to go to the assistance of any imperilled mariners.

After supper he accompanied Abner to the little landing where a stout rowboat was fastened.

Into this they dropped, and Darry immediately seized upon the oars, to the secret amusement and satisfaction of the life saver, who was quite willing to let him display his ability in this important line.

"Yuh sure pull a good, strong stroke, lad," he declared, after they had been upon the bay for some time, Darry taking his bearings from a bright star that had appeared in the east.

"He taught me," replied the boy, and, perhaps unconsciously, his voice quavered as he spoke, for he could not even think of the captain without emotion.

"All the better. A feller ain't no use 'round this section less he kin row a boat with the best. And if so be yuh 'spect to jine with us some day, the more yuh larn about this same thing the better for yuh. Joe, he was a reg'lar water duck—but he was too darin' and he tried the game onct too often. Beware o' that inlet, lad. The tide sweeps outen it like a mill race sometimes, an' the best man couldn't hold his own agin it. It's ben a mystery to me always how it happened. Nobody ever knowed, only that we found the boat two days arter on the beach, three miles up. When yuh git tired say so, an' I'll spell yuh."

After a long time they drew near the other shore. Here lights had been seen, and Darry discovered quite a collection of houses, for the most part cabins such as are so common in the south, especially along the coast of North Carolina.

Abner insisted upon taking the oars now; and as he knew just where it was most desirable to land the boy no longer objected.

Sitting there in the stern he watched the scene unfold as they approached the mainland, though the new moon gave very little light.

Sounds as of boys at play, together with the barking of dogs, and even the gabble of a goose, awoke in his breast new emotions such as he had never experienced before; for he was about to be introduced to a home, no matter of what character, where he would after that belong.

The boat was brought up against a landing, and both went ashore.

"In the mornin' I'll get yuh to help carry the groceries to the boat, so I kin ferry 'em acrost. Jest now I'm pinin' to get to the shack, 'cause I ain't ben home these two weeks, yuh see. This way, Darry, lad. My cabin ain't jest in the village; but when I come home I ginerally stop in at the butcher's an' take some meat along. Git out, yuh yaller critter!" this to a dog that had come barking toward them as though recognizing the fact that a stranger had come to town.

"Hyar, Peake, don't yer hit my dorg!" shouted a half-grown boy, slouching around a corner as though he had just come out of a drinking resort there.

"Keep him home, then, Jim Dilks, er else teach the critter to behave. He tackled me onct and I had to kick him over a fence to save my shins from his teeth. Some day that hound'll get a call all right, yuh hear me, Jim?" declared Abner.

Jim leered at him, and then looked at the boy.

"Reckon it'll be a bad day for the feller that hurts me dorg, see? Who yer got trailin' 'long with yer, Peake? Say, be he the critter as kim ashore? Sooner he skips outen this the better. We ain't got jobs enough now fur them as growed up round hyar."

"No danger of you worrin' 'bout jobs, Jim Dilks. Work an' you never got on well. Mind your own business, now. This lad can look out for hisself. He's goin' to live with me. Come on, Darry, don't notice the loafer," concluded the life saver; and he and the boy passed on. Darry was destined to see a great deal more of Jim Dilks, as we shall presently learn.

CHAPTER IV: THE CABIN BY THE MARSH

As is customary in many of these little villages along the coast, the butcher shop was also the country store where groceries, dry goods, notions, and possibly boots and hats in addition, were sold.

Mr. Keeler eyed the boy in Abner's company, while he was cutting off the meat.

"Likely lad, that, Mr. Peake," he said. "I reckon he must be the one that come ashore from the wreck t'other night. I heard all about it, 'cause some of our men were over to help out," he added, in a low tone, taking advantage of Darry straying off a bit to examine a colored print that hung on the wall, and offered all manner of inducements to young fellows wishing to enlist in the navy.

"The boy's all right. He's gwine to live with my missus—if they kin git on together. But about them as were over, Gus, I've got a notion some on 'em thought it might be a good chanct to wreck a craft. I seen Dilks there, with his crowd, an' yuh know he's under suspicion o' havin' lured that schooner ashore with a false light last year. Time's comin' when them rascals air goin' to git caught. Hangin' 'd be too easy for such snakes. An' that boy o' his'n promises to be a chip o' the ole block. He's as bad as they make 'em," returned the surfman, shaking his head.

Nothing so angers a life saver as the mention of a wrecker; for deep down in his heart he believes that the men who make a living from salvage after a vessel has gone to pieces on the reefs, or else in boarding the wreck when the storm has gone down, would not hesitate a minute about sending any ship to her doom if they believed it could be done without too much risk.

"If he doesn't get on with the missus let me have a try with him, Abner. Looks to be a likely lad. They're a scarce article around here—some go to sea, others are in the service, and more get drowned; while those that are left seem bad from top to bottom, just like Jim Dilks. Yes, I could use that younker, I think."

Peake had turned white at mention of the fate that befalls so many young men of the shore; but he made no remark concerning his feelings.

"I'll remember what yuh say, Mr. Keeler. But I got a notion the boy will stick with me. When the missus gets to know him she can't help but like him. He's the clear quill. Take the change out of that bill. We just got paid last night, yuh see. Darry, let's move along."

The village merchant looked after the couple a little enviously, as though something about the boy's appearance had awakened his interest.

"I saw Jim Dilks talking to Peake before they came in here. I wager that young scamp has it in for the new boy in town. He's been a holy terror for a long time, and for one I think something should be done to put a stop to his doings. But his father has a grip on the worst elements here, and everyone seems afraid to rile up the old wrecker. Some say he used to be a smuggler years back, and even blacker stories are told of his life in Cuba, before Spain got out of the island. Well, it's none of my business. I don't dare act alone. If someone else starts the ball rolling I'll give it a big shove." And so the butcher salved his conscience for not doing his duty.

Meanwhile Darry and his new friend walked briskly along, talking as they went.

The boy had seen considerable of foreign ports, and the many strange things he could tell were doubly interesting to this simple life saver, who had never been further than to Wilmington in all his life.

"See that light ahead, lad? That's a lamp in the windy o' my shack. They knows when my night comes around, an' the missus puts that lamp there. It's a big thing, Darry, to have a light in the windy, ashinin' only fur you. Makes a feller feel like he had one leetle nest in all this big world, where some un cared fur him. And that is goin' to be your home too, boy."

"I don't know how to thank you, Mr. Peake," faltered the lad.

"Then don't try. Besides, mebbe yuh won't like it so well, after all. Nancy, she ain't so easy to get on with, since leetle Joe went away. Seems like she jest can't ever git over it. I seen her cryin' the last time I was over. No use tryin' to comfort the pore ole gal. It left a sore place in her heart that nothin' kin ever heal. I'm a hopin' that p'haps with you around she may perk up some."

They were soon at the door. It was thrown open at the sound of Abner's call, and two rather unkempt little girls rushed out, to be tossed up in the air by the proud father.

They looked at Darry with wide-eyed wonder, for strangers were uncommon in this neighborhood, so far removed from the railroad.

"Come right in, Darry. Here's the missus," said the life saver.

A woman came forward, and after greeting Abner, looked with a little frown in the direction of the boy.

The surfman hastened to explain that Darry was a survivor of the last wreck, on the shore where so many brave ships had left their bones.

"He's a waif, what's never knowed no home, Nance. The captain picked him up abroad, but he's English or American, sure enough. With the death of that captain went his only friend. I liked the lad,—he somehow made me think of our Joe. Jest the same size, too, and he could wear his clothes fine. He'd be a great help to yuh, I reckons, if so be yuh would like to have him stay."

Abner saw a look of coming trouble in the eyes of his wife, and his voice took on a pleading tone.

His mention of Joe was unfortunate, perhaps, for the woman had never become reconciled to the loss of her only boy, and always declared Heaven had dealt unjustly with her when there were so many worthless lads in the village, who could have been far better spared.

"Just like I didn't have my hands full now, without bringing home any more mouths to feed," she fumed. "Like as not he's a good-for-nothing like Jim Dilks, and will only make us trouble right along. Keep him over at the station if you want, Abner Peake, but you don't quarter him on me. This is my house, and I'm to be consulted before anybody is brought here."

Abner had apparently thought this all over.

He simply took Darry's hand and drew the half resisting lad over in front of the irate woman.

"Nancy, I never knowed yuh to be anything but fair. S'posin' our leetle Joe was kerried out to sea, an' in a strange land met up with a citizen as took him home to his wife. What kinder reception do yuh think he'd get? Could any woman look in Joe's face an' send him away from her door? Wall, then, jest look in the face o' this boy, an' then if so be yuh say take him away, I'll do it, Nancy," he said, simply.

Almost against her will she was compelled to look.

Well it was for Darry that he had clear eyes in which lurked no guile, for that gaze of the surfman's "missus" was searching, since she had before her mind a picture of the lost Joe.

She only nodded her head and said:

"Let him stay."

Perhaps she was too full of emotion to say more; but the husband nodded his head as though satisfied with what he had done.

"It's all right, boy; she seen Joey in your eyes, jest as I done. Seems to me yuh kin make good with the ole woman. Don't notice all she says fur a time. Sure she's suffered some."

Apparently the family had waited with supper for Abner to come home, for his wife immediately placed the meat on the frying pan, and the odor of steak quickly filled every cranny of the small cabin of three rooms.

The two little girls were slow to make up with Darry, but he knew how to interest them in certain ways, and it was not long before they hovered around him as if he were a curiosity indeed.

Abner tried to make himself as agreeable as possible, for various reasons.

He saw that his wife had not yet become reconciled to the fact of a stranger coming among them, and was watching Darry out of the corners of her eyes from time to time, while a frown would gather on her brow.

She was a sharp-featured woman; but life goes hard with those of her sex in this coast country, and they grow old at forty.

Darry was studying hard how to please her, for he felt that she was to be pitied after having lost her only boy so suddenly a year or so back; and he determined never to forget this if she should scold him needlessly or show temper.

He anticipated her wants in the line of wood for the fire, cheerfully assisted in washing up the supper dishes, and was withal so obliging that ere long the anxious Abner saw the lines begin to leave the forehead of his better half.

This tickled him more than any well-won fight in the breakers might have done, for he had a secret dread of Nancy's often ungovernable temper.

"The boy's gone and done it, blame me if he ain't!" he muttered to himself, when he saw his wife actually smile over at where Darry was sitting, with one of the twins on either side, entranced with some figures he was drawing to illustrate a little story he had been telling them about some sight seen in Naples.

When it came time to retire Darry was given a shake-down in the second room.

He felt that he had made some sort of an impression upon the surfman's wife, and that after all she might not prove so hard to win as he had feared from what little he had heard about her temper.

That night was the most peaceful he had known for some time.

In the morning he was up before any one else stirred, and when Mrs Peake made her appearance she found a bright fire burning in the kitchen, plenty of wood on hand, a bucket of water from the spring handy, and a boy only too anxious to do anything he was told in the way of chores.

Perhaps she may have had a suspicion that it would not last.

"A new broom sweeps clean," she remarked to Abner, as he appeared and looked at her inquiringly.

"I calkerlate this one means to keep a-going' right along," he said, "yuh see, the poor critter ain't never had no home before, an' he'll sorter 'preciate one now. Give him a show an' he'll make good."

When Abner had to return to the other side of the bay Darry went with him to the store, where a supply of edibles was laid in according to the list written out by the station keeper; together with a can of oil, since their stock had run low.

When Abner shook his hand heartily at pushing off, Darry felt as though another link connecting him with the past had been broken.

Perhaps his face betrayed his feelings, for the old man exclaimed:

"Keep a stiff upper lip, lad, and it'll all come out well. The missus is interested in yuh already. Tell her that I said to give yuh Joe's gun, and the traps he left. He writ down how he used to git the muskrats an' coons, too, so yuh kin understand how to set the traps. Tell the missus that yuh mean to share an' share alike with her in the money yuh get. That'll please her, 'cause yuh see cash is some skeerce with we-'uns all the time. Ten dollars a week don't go far. Sometimes Nancy hunts roots in the marshes, or picks up a few turkles that sells for a dollar or two each. To-morrow yuh bring over the mail. I've got a boat as is fair, if it only had a new pair o' oars. P'raps as a sailor lad yuh could whittle out a pair to answer. Well, good-bye, Darry, my boy, and good luck. Keep an eye out to windward for squalls if so be that Jim Dilks shows alongside."

When the surfman had pulled with a strong stroke for some distance he paused long enough to wave his hand to the boy; after which Darry turned away to get the articles Mrs. Peake wanted at the store, and for which she had doled out the necessary cash to a penny.

It would seem as though Abner must have had a vision of some coming trouble in connection with the ne'er-do-well son of the notorious wrecker, Dilks, for even as Darry entered the village street on his way to the general store he saw the heavily built young ruffian shuffling toward him.

There was a leer on the features of the bully.

Our hero had knocked around the world long enough to be able to detect signs of a coming storm when he saw them; and if ever the signals were set for trouble they certainly gave evidence of being now, when that shiftless Jim Dilks intercepted the newcomer.

CHAPTER V: AN ENCOUNTER ON THE ROAD

Jim Dilks had long ruled as the bully of Ashley village.

He had a reputation as a bad boy that served him in place of fighting; and as a rule an angry word from him was sufficient to command obedience.

Besides, Nature had made him so ugly that when he scowled it was enough to send a shiver down the spinal column of most boys.

Darry came to a pause. Indeed, he could not well have continued along the path he was taking without walking over the bully, so completely had Jim blocked his way.

"Looky here, didn't yer hear me tell yer last night ter get outen this place?" demanded the wrecker's son, thrusting that aggressive chin of his forward still more, and glaring at his prospective victim in his usual commanding way.

"I believe you did say something like that. Are you Jim Dilks?" asked Darry, and to the surprise of the other he did not seem to show the customary anxiety that went with hostile demonstrations by the bully.

"When air yer going, then?" continued Jim.

"I haven't decided. In fact, I like my present accommodations with Mrs. Peake so well that I may stay there right along," replied Darry, steadily.

Jim caught his breath, and in such a noisy way that one would think it was a porpoise blowing in the inlet.

In all his experience he had never come across such an experience as this.

"I see yer want takin' down," he cried. "I've run this ranch a long time now, an' there ain't no new feller comin' here without I say so. Yer got ter skip out er take a lickin' on the spot. Now, I give yer one more chanct ter say yer'll hoof it."

Darry knew what it meant, for he had not knocked around so long without learning the signs of storm and fight.

He had thought seriously over this very matter, after being warned that he might sooner or later have trouble with Jim; and as a result his decision was already formed.

When Jim Dilks saw him deliberately taking off his jacket he stared, with a new sensation beginning to make its presence felt around the region of his heart—the element of uncertainty, even fear.

"Wot yer doin' that fur?" he demanded, shaking his head after the manner of a pugnacious rooster about to enter into combat for the mastery of the barnyard.

"Why, you said you were going to lick me, and as this is a very good coat Mrs. Peake gave me, one that used to belong to her boy, Joe, I thought she might feel bad if she saw it dusty or torn," replied Darry, solemnly.

"Say, you bean't goin' ter fight, be yer?" gasped Jim, hardly able to believe his senses, the shock was so great.

"Why, you said I had to. I don't want to fight a bit, but I always obey orders, you see, and you told me I must or leave Ashley. Now, I don't mean to go away, so I suppose I must do the other thing. But I hate to hurt anyone."

"Hey? You hurt me? Don't worry about thet, cub. I reckon I kin wipe up the ground with a feller o' yer build. So yer won't run, eh? Then all I kin say is yer got to take yer medicine, see?"

Naturally, Jim knew next to nothing about the science of boxing, for he had always depended upon his brute strength to pull him through, backed by his really ferocious appearance, when he assumed his "fighting face," as he was proudly wont to term it.

On the other hand Darry had often boxed during the dog watch, with some of the sailors aboard the old brigantine, and since there were several among the crew who prided themselves on a knowledge of fisticuffs, he imbibed more or less of skill in the dexterity shown in both self defense and aggressive tactics.

At the same time Darry had seldom been called upon to utilize this knowledge, for he was of a peaceful nature, and would shun a fight if it could be done in honor.

Now, he knew that Jim Dilks was determined to have it out with him, and consequently, if he really intended to remain in Ashley, he must show this bully that he could take care of himself.

Jim was surprised when he received a staggering blow in the first encounter, and before he had even been able to lay a hand on his antagonist, who, after striking had nimbly bounded aside, so that the village boy came near falling down.

Believing that this must have been only an accident, Jim turned with a roar and once more strove to crush his rival by sheer weight and bulldog tactics.

There never was a fight yet that did not immediately attract a crowd of the curious and idle. Boys came running from several quarters, and not a few men too, the more shame to them, always glad to watch a contest, whether between a pair of aggressive dogs or roosters, or pugnacious lads.

Those who came running up could hardly believe their eyes, when they saw the recognized bully of the village engaged with a strange boy, and apparently, thus far, getting the worst of the bargain.

Darry felt rather ashamed to be caught in the centre of such a gathering; but the fight had been forced upon him, and the only thing left was to wind it up as quickly as possible.

Accordingly, he began to force matters, and the third time that Jim leaped at him, failing as before to land his blow, he received a sudden shock in the shape of a swift tap directly under the ear that hurled him to the ground.

There was a buzz of excitement about this time.

Boys who had tamely yielded to the sway of the bully for many moons began to take notice, and even say things that were not calculated to soothe the lacerated feelings of Jim who was picking himself up slowly, and trying to collect his scattered wits.

The bully, of course, had not had enough as yet. This time, however, when he came on it was with considerable caution, for his rough experience had begun to teach him that rush tactics were not going to answer with the boy who knew so well how to handle his fists.

It made no difference, for Darry met him squarely, and after a rapid interchange of blows that brought out many a whoop from those who looked on, Jim once more received an unexpected tap that caused him to sit down a second time.

He was in no hurry to get up now, but sat there in a half-dazed way, rubbing the side of his head, and gritting his teeth savagely.

The crowd began to cheer, and it must have been a galling sound to that defeated bully, whose hour had come, as it usually does with most of his kind.

"Get up!" said one man, jeeringly.

Jim scrambled to his feet, to find his antagonist facing him in a manner that made him quail.

"Are you done, or shall we go on with it?" asked Darry, calmly, for he did not seem to have been even winded in the exchange of blows.

"Ah, git out. Me hand is sprained, I tell ye. I fell on it last night. That's why I couldn't knock yer out. This thing ain't done yet, cub. I'll git yer as sure as me name is Jim Dilks. I allers do wen I goes arter a feller."

He turned away with his head tossed in the air as though victory had really perched upon his banner.

HE WAS IN NO HURRY TO GET UP NOW, BUT SAT THERE IN A HALF-DAZED WAY.

The laugh that arose must have been galling to his pride, for he stopped in his tracks and looked around angrily in the hopes of detecting one of the boys in the act, whom he could trash later on as a sop to his wounded feelings; but they were shrewd enough to hide their exultant faces just then.

Darry picked up his coat, and putting it on, strode away.

He was conscious of a feeling of satisfaction, not because he had whipped his antagonist, for it had been almost too easy; but he knew Jim Dilks had long lorded it over the boys of Ashley, and perhaps after this he might hesitate to act the part of bully again.

At any rate he was not intending to leave the place just because one fellow had given him orders; perhaps before they left him alone he might have to repeat this dose; but the reputation of the one who had downed Jim Dilks would travel fast, and the balance of the village herd would think twice before trying conclusions with the new boy at Peake's.

CHAPTER VI: WINNING HIS WAY

When Darry entered the store the proprietor looked at him with interest.

Mr. Keeler was a very strait-laced individual, and wont to raise his hands in horror at the mention of fighting, or anything, in fact, that partook of violence. He always gave it as his opinion that football was a brutal game, equal to the bull rights of the Spaniards, and could hardly be induced to even watch a baseball match, for fear one of the players be injured.

Nevertheless, Mr. Keeler was human, and from the door of his shop he had seen the little affair on the road, and recognized the combatants as Peake's new boy and the village bully.

He could hardly believe his eyes when he saw that Darry had come off victor, and that the idle men who gaped at the encounter were giving Jim the laugh as he crossly slouched away.

Perhaps after all there might be something in such a fight as this, where a much-needed lesson was taught a young scoundrel.

Mr. Keeler had his eyes opened for once; but at the same time he thought it his duty as a man of peace to speak to the new boy.

"What was the trouble about, my lad?" he asked, as Darry handed him a list of the articles Mrs. Peake wished him to bring back.

"There was no trouble on my side. I only wanted to be left alone, sir," replied our hero, smiling.

"Oh! I see, and Jim wouldn't have it? Like as not he told you to get off the earth—it would be just like his impudence."

"Not quite so bad as that, sir, but he did say I couldn't stay with Mrs. Peake, and must move on. I'm quite satisfied where I am, and I mean to stay—that is as long as she wants me to."

"Quite right. I suppose there may be times when a boy is compelled to stand up for his rights, although I've generally preached the other way. But if you had to fight I'm glad you succeeded in convincing Jim that you could hold your own."

"That was easy enough, sir. He is a clumsy fighter."

"I hope you do not love to engage in such affairs, Darry?" continued the grocer, alive to what he considered his duty.

"I've been set upon a few times when I had to defend myself, but I never look for trouble. I'd even avoid it if I could; but you know, Mr. Keeler, sometimes a boy has to either run away or fight; and somehow I don't care to run away."

Mr. Keeler nodded his head.

He was getting a new insight into boy character that day, that might revolutionize a few of his pet theories.

"You say you have decided to stay with the Peakes?" he continued.

"If Mrs. Peake wants me to. It isn't quite decided yet; but I think I shall like to have a home there. You see, sir, outside of the cabin of the old Falcon I've never known a home in all my life."

Mr. Keeler felt a new interest in this strange lad, who had been a wanderer the brief span of his days, and yet strange to say seemed to possess the instincts of a manly young chap.

He wondered very much where the boy could have picked up his ways; but then Mr. Keeler had never met Captain Harley, or he might not have indulged in so much vague speculation.

"If you can get on with Mrs. Peake you deserve considerable praise, lad. Not but what she is a good enough woman, and with a kindly heart; but ever since little Joe went out on the ebb tide and never came back again she seems to have become what I might say, soured on humanity. Abner is meek enough to stand it, but she has had quarrels with many people in the village. Still, who knows but what you may be the very one to do her good. You are about the size of her Joe, and with his clothes on, I declare now, you do look a little like him. He was a clever boy, and I just reckon her heart was all wrapped up in him. At any rate, I wish you success there, Darry. And if I can do you a good turn at any time just ask me."

"Thank you, sir," replied the boy, with a lump in his throat; for he was unused to kindness save from Captain Harley, and had had more hard knocks in the past than good wishes.

The benevolent grocer continued to chat with him until the purchases were all tied up in a bundle, and after payment had been made Darry placed the rather bulky package on his shoulder and trotted off.

On the way home he was not spoken to by anyone.

He saw several boys pointing in his direction, and there was a look of awe on their faces as they watched him walk by; but no one ventured to address a word to the newcomer who was said to have roundly trounced big Jim.

A tall man also looked sharply at him, and as he wore a great nickel star on the breast of his coat Darry understood that this must be Hank Squires, the constable of the village.

No doubt news of the encounter had drifted to his ears, and since the boy who usually made life miserable for him had come out "second best" Hank did not think it policy to take any official notice of the misdemeanor.

As soon as he arrived at home, Darry busied himself in undoing his package, and placing the various articles where Mrs. Peake told him they belonged.

His manner was so obliging and his answers to her questions so ready, that despite her feeling of resentment at Abner, thinking anyone could ever take the place of Joe in her heart, the woman found herself insensibly drawn to the boy.

Perhaps, after all, the mere fact that he had never known a mother's love, nor had a home of any kind, appealed more to her sympathies than anything else.

She watched him take off his coat and carefully fold it before setting to work.

That too, was like Joe, always trying to save his mother needless worry and work.

After a while, as he happened to come close to her in doing something to save her steps, she uttered a little exclamation.

"Did you fall down with the bundle, Darry?" she asked, leaning forward.

He turned a little red, conscious that in some way she must have discovered signs of his recent adventure on the road.

"Oh! no, it was not heavy at all, ma'am," he replied, and then noting that her eyes were fastened on his cheek he put up his hand, in this way discovering for the first time, a little soreness there.

When he withdrew his fingers he saw a spot of blood.

"How did that happen then, Darry?" she asked, suspiciously.

"I think he must have hit me there, but I didn't know it until now," he replied, relieved to feel that he could tell her the whole truth.

"Someone struck you—have you been fighting then?" she asked, a little coldly; for woman-like, Mrs. Peake did not approve of strenuous encounters.

"He said that I would have to leave you, and get out. I couldn't do anything else but defend myself when he came at me. I'm sorry, for I never tried to get in a fight in my life, and I never ran away from one either."

"Who was it, Darry?" she asked again, looking uneasy.

"Jim Dilks," he answered promptly, unconsciously squaring his shoulders.

"Oh! that terrible boy again! What a shame he can't pick out some one of his own size to beat! Did he hurt you very much, my poor boy?"

Then she was surprised to see Darry smile broadly.

"I didn't know he had even struck me until just now. You see Captain Harley allowed me to box with the sailors, and I learned how to defend myself. Jim says he is going to get even with me later on," he said modestly.

"Do you mean to tell me you whipped that big loafer, that good-for-nothing bully who has run the place for years?" exclaimed the woman, in astonishment.

"I wouldn't just say that, ma'am, and Jim wouldn't admit it either; but I did knock him down twice, and the second time he said he wouldn't fight any more because, you see, his right hand was sprained. So he went off and left me alone."

"Splendid! He deserved a lesson, the brute! Many's the time he has jeered at me when he passed; and everyone has been afraid to put a hand on him because his father is a bad man. And you did that? Well, the boys of Ashley ought to vote you thanks. And you fought because he wanted you to leave this house? You thought it was a home worth fighting for? Then it shall be yours as long as you want to stay here, Darry."

Before he suspected how greatly her feelings had been aroused, Mrs. Peake threw her arms about his neck and gave him a resounding kiss—perhaps in her heart she was in this way demonstrating her undying affection for the boy who had vanished from that home one year ago, and never came back.

After that Darry worked with a light heart, such as he had never before known in all his life.

During the afternoon Abner's wife took pains to open a box that contained all the treasured possessions of the young trapper and naturalist whose greatest delight had been to spend his time in the swamps watching the animals at their play; and in the proper season setting his traps to secure the pelts of muskrats, 'coons and skunks, which, properly cured, would bring high prices at such centres where furs are collected, and secure many little luxuries for his mother during the winter season.

Darry handled these with a bit of reverence, for he knew what a wrench it must be to the devoted heart of the mother to see a stranger touching the things she had hoarded up as treasures, and over which she must have had many a secret cry.

Together with the traps and other things there was an old shotgun still in good condition, and Darry had visions of coming days in the marsh and swamp, where fat ducks and squirrels might fall to his aim, and provide good dinners for this little family into whose humble home he had now been fully taken.

His heart was filled with gratitude, for he knew that his lines had fallen in pleasant places, since he was no longer a waif in the world.

CHAPTER VII: THE MIDNIGHT ALARM

Darry found himself greatly interested in the little diary left behind by the boy naturalist, and which, besides containing an account of his catches in the way of fur-bearing animals, also explained his methods of setting snares and traps, how he cured the skins when taken, and where he received the highest prices for the same.

All of this information was eagerly devoured by his successor, who felt that it was certainly up to him to do his share toward supporting the little family of the life saver who had been so kind to him.

He wandered out late one afternoon to look around and see what prospect there might be for game; since the fall season was now on, and the boom of guns beginning to be heard on the bay, where the ducks were commencing to congregate.

As he drew near the cabin just at dusk he was surprised to discover a figure making off in a suspicious way, as though not desirous of being seen.

He recognized the lurker as Jim Dilks, and the fact gave him considerable uneasiness, for he had not forgotten how the other vowed to get even for his discomfiture, and Jim's methods of wiping out a score were sometimes little short of shocking, if Darry could believe half he had heard.

Had the fellow been prowling around in hopes of meeting him again, and trying conclusions a second time?

Darry could not believe it, for such a thing would not be in line with the reputation of the village bully.

He would be more apt to try and obtain a mean revenge by doing some injury to the kind woman who had given refuge to this shipwrecked lad.

Evidently Mrs. Peake should know what he had seen, and so as soon as he entered the kitchen, he spoke of it.

"Jim Dilks hanging about here," she echoed, in rising anger; "I'd just like to know what that scamp wants, that's all. No good follows his visits, as every one about this section knows to their sorrow."

"I'm afraid I'm the cause of it all. Unfortunately my being here is apt to bring trouble down upon you. Perhaps it might be as well if I moved on, as he said," remarked the boy, dejectedly.

The woman looked at him quickly, almost sharply.

"Do you want to go?" she demanded.

"No, oh, never; but it would save you trouble, and I have no right to bring that on you," he cried, hastily, and with emotion.

"Then I say you shan't go away, not for a dozen Jim Dilks. You belong here now. I've done what I said I never would do, given away my Joey's things, and you're my boy, I say. I won't let you go away! This is your home as long as you want to stay. Let me catch that Jim Dilks trying to chase you off, that's all."

Darry could not trust his voice to say one word, only caught up her work-stained hand and pressed it to his lips, then fled from the house.

And yet as Darry stood out under the old oak that shielded the cottage from the burning sun in summer, and the biting winds of the "northers" in winter, looking up at the first bright evening star that peeped into view, he felt a happiness deep down in his boyish heart that could not be excelled by a prince of the royal blood coming into his palace home.

He was merry all evening, and the twins romped as they had not done for many a day, in fact, ever since their brother had left them.

The mother looked on in silent approval, thinking that once more home seemed to have a brightness about it that had been long lacking.

When all had retired save Darry he sat by the fire thinking.

Somehow he could not forget that skulking figure he had seen leaving the vicinity of the cabin at dusk, and he would have given much to have known just what mission brought the vindictive Jim out there.

The bully's home was in the village, and he had no business so far away, unless bent on an errand that would not bear the light of day.

A sense of responsibility came upon the boy as he sat there.

What if this young wretch should be cruel enough to poison the chickens, or the three pigs that were expected to help carry the family over the winter?

The thought gave him a bad feeling, and almost unconsciously he reached out his hand and picked up the gun that Joe had purchased with money earned through the sale of roots dug in the woods or furs secured through clever deadfalls.

There were a few shells in the box, and among others, several containing very small shot, that might sting pretty lively, but could not do much damage to a half-grown boy as tough as Jim Dilks.

And it was with that same individual in his mind that Darry pushed two of these small bird shells into the barrels of the gun.

He did not know that he would care to send even this charge directly at a human being; but in case it became necessary he wanted to make certain he would do little harm.

After that he seemed to feel easier in his mind, for he lay down and was soon fast asleep.

Something awoke him about midnight, and thinking he had heard a sound he sat up to listen; then he heard it again, and felt sure it must be a cough, as of some one partly choking.

He was worried and left his lowly bed to go to the door connecting the rooms and listen, but nothing came from beyond.

Could the sound come from outside?

He slipped on some of his clothes, and stepping over quietly opened the outer door, looking into the night.

The new moon had long since vanished behind the horizon, and yet he could see some sort of flickering light, coming from that region back of the house.

At the same time he believed he caught the muttering of voices, or it might be a low chuckle, followed by a plain sneeze.

Smoke came to his nostrils, and that meant fire!

Darry had a sudden vision of Jim Dilks getting even, and it took the form of a burning corn-crib or chicken house.

Filled with indignation, he turned back into the house, and snatched up the old shotgun; gone now was his hesitation with regard to using the gun to pepper the rascally gang that took orders from the even more rascally Jim.

Without saying a word Darry shot out of the door and turned the corner, when his worst fears were realized, for he saw flames rising up alongside the pigsty, which adjoined the building in which the fowls were kept.

His first act was to fire the right barrel of his gun in the air, and at the same time give vent to a shout.

Immediately several shadowy figures, which in spite of their bent attitudes he knew to be boys, started to scamper away, in sudden alarm lest they be recognized, and made to pay the penalty in the squire's court.

As near as Darry could tell there were three of them, and as they ran he believed he could recognize Jim Dilks in the centre of the group.

The temptation was too great to be resisted, and filled with indignation because of the cowardly trick of which they had been guilty, Darry took a snap shot at the running bunch.

It was music to his ears to catch the howls that immediately arose; but he knew no serious damage had resulted because they ran faster than ever after that, quickly vanishing from view in the shadows.

There was work to be done if he would save the humble quarters of the family porkers from destruction, and the hennery as well.

He knew where the rain barrel stood that held the wash water, and snatching up a bucket he hastily dipped it in, after which he rushed over to the fire and dashed the contents upon the blaze.

Back and forth he galloped, using considerable discretion as to where he put the water so as to head off the creeping fire.

Mrs. Peake now came running with another bucket, and proved herself a woman in a thousand by assisting the new addition to the family put out the last of the conflagration.

When there was not a spark remaining, and beyond the grunting of the pigs and the cackling of the fowls, everything had fallen back into its usual condition, one or two neighbors arrived on the scene, asking questions, and busying themselves generally, though had it depended on their efforts the frail buildings must have gone up in smoke before now.

Of course many questions were fired at Darry, and he felt that it was necessary he should tell what he had seen, though cautious about saying he had fully recognized any one of the three skulkers, no matter what strong suspicions he may have entertained.

He believed he had a means of identifying one or more of them, nevertheless, when the proper time came.

More neighbors arrived, attracted by the shots and the confusion, for nothing could quiet the excited chickens; and for an hour there was more or less discussion on the part of these good people.

Finally the excitement died out, the last neighbor went home, and the Peake cabin was left to those who belonged there. There was no further alarm during the balance of that eventful night.

CHAPTER VIII: ACROSS THE BAY

Darry welcomed the coming of dawn.

He was glad to see that the sky was clear, for he anticipated a long row across the broad bay that day, bearing the mail for those at the life-saving station, as well as several things he had been commissioned to fetch over by Abner.

Hardly had they finished breakfast than there arrived a visitor.

Mrs. Peake saw him coming along the road, for she could look out of the window of the kitchen, where they ate, and have a view of the open stretch.

"Here comes old Hank Squires. I reckon he's heard something about what happened here last night. It's about time he took notice of some of the mean pranks those village boys play on those who live outside. Tell him all he wants to hear, Darry; but unless you can swear to it perhaps you'd better not say that you think it was Jim Dilks and his crowd. If you feel sure, go ahead," she remarked, for with all her temper Mrs. Peake was a woman with a due sense of caution.

The constable knocked, and in response to her call to "come in," he entered.

"I heard ye had a little shindig up to here last night, Mrs. Peake, an' I jest called 'round to see what it is all 'bout," said Hank, seating himself. "I see thar was a fire here all right, an' it kim near burning yer buildings down in the bargain. Some says as how it was sot by a passel o' boys. How 'bout that, ma'am?"

"I didn't see anyone," answered the woman. "When I got out Darry here had the fire pretty well under control, and I only helped him finish. You can ask him about it, Mr. Squires."

Darry had already learned through the grocer that previous to her marriage to Abner the good woman had been for some years a teacher in the schools, which fact accounted for her superior language and knowledge of things that were far above the intelligence of most of her neighbors.

The constable looked keenly at our hero.

"I b'lieve this is the boy wot was saved from the wreck o' that brigantine. So he's gwine to be your boy now, Mrs. Peake? Well, I understand he's got the makin' o' a man in him, so Mr. Keeler sez to me last night, and I hope you'll never have no reason to be sorry. I want to know, Darry, what about this here fire?"

"I'll be only too glad to tell you all I know, sir," replied the boy promptly.

"When did it happen?" began the constable, with the air of a famous lawyer, with a bewildered witness on the rack.

"I think it was somewhere near midnight. I have no watch, and Mrs. Peake took the little clock in her room with her."

"That was near the time. It was half-past one when I went back to my bed with my two little girls," remarked the owner of the house.

"S'pose you tell me what happened, jest as it comes to you, lad."

With this invitation Darry soon related the whole matter, even to his firing after the vanishing culprits.

This latter event appeared to interest the constable more than anything else.

"Do you think you hit any o' 'em?" he asked, eagerly.

"They didn't stop to tell me, but I heard a lot of howling, and they ran faster than ever," replied Darry, smiling.

"That sounds as if you did some damage. Mrs. Peake, I must look into this outrage closer, and if I can only git my hands on any dead-sure evidence somebody's boys is a gwine to pay for the fiddlin'. I'm tired o' sech goings-on. They sure are a disgrace to our village. But you know how it is—my hands are tied acause theys politics back o' it all. If I arrested Jim Dilks now on the strength o' a suspicion I'd get tied up in litigation and lose my job in the bargain. I hears as how theys gwine to be a meetin' called at the house o' the dominie to discuss this question, an' see what kin be did to change things."

"I'm sure I'm glad to know it, and if they want another to join in tell them to count on Nancy Peake. The women must take this thing in hand, since the men are too much afraid of that ruffian, big Jim Dilks, to do anything. Be sure and let me know when that meeting is coming off, Mr. Squires," said Abner's better half; and when he saw the fire in her eyes and the determination shining there Constable Squires realized that the day of salvation for Ashley village was not so very far away.

"Then you wouldn't like to swear to its being any particular pusson?" he went on, turning again to Darry.

"I did not see a face, and without that my evidence would hardly convict. No, sir, I would not swear that one of the three was Jim."

"That's bad. I stand ready to do my duty and arrest the boy if so be any one makes a complaint; but without that it wouldn't pay and only makes useless trouble all 'round. But I'm goin' to keep my eyes open from now on, and when I git a sure case on Jim he comes in."

That was all Mr. Squires would say, and he soon departed; but not before he had called Darry outside for a few words in parting.

"Looks like you was marked to be the central figger o' the comin' storm, lad. Keep your eye open for squalls. If things git too black around jest slip over to the dominie's leetle house and hev a talk with him. I knows more about what's gwine to happen than I let on; but somebody's due to hev a surprise that hain't a donation party either. You seem to have the right stuff in you, lad. I heard from Mr. Keeler how you took that bully Jim into camp mighty neat. He'll never be satisfied till he's paid you back. A word to the wise is sufficient. Goodbye, Darry."

After all the constable did not seem to be a bad sort of fellow.

During the morning Darry accomplished many things for Abner's wife, and she showed in her manner how pleased she was to have him there.

When noon had come and gone he prepared for his row across the bay, for she insisted upon his making an early start.

"Clouds are banking up in the southeast, and we look for trouble whenever that comes about. Still, you will have plenty of time to row over. Stay with Abner to-night and return in the morning if it is safe on the bay. Perhaps you may have a chance to see how the life savers work," said Mrs. Peake.

It was almost two when he pushed off from the float and started on his long row directly across the bay.

Steadily he kept pushing across the wide stretch of shallow water.

As Abner had said, a new pair of oars seemed to be badly needed in connection with the old boat; but a willing heart and sturdy arms sent the craft along until finally Darry reached his goal.

The storm was drawing near, for by now the heavens were clouded over, and the haze seemed to thicken. Perhaps had he lingered another hour Darry might have stood a chance of losing his way, and being drawn out of the inlet by the powerful ebb tide—just as the unfortunate Joe had been.

Abner was waiting at the landing for him.

"Glad to see yuh, lad. How's everything to home?" he asked.

Of course Darry understood this to mean with regard to himself and his relations with the good woman of the house.

Truth to tell Abner had worried more than a little since parting from the boy, for his wife had shown more than unusual ill temper lately, and he feared that he had possibly done an unwise thing in leaving Darry there to be a constant reminder of the son she had lost.

But the happy look on the boy's countenance eased his mind even before the boy spoke a single word.

"He kin do it, if any boy kin," was what the life saver was saying under his breath.

"All well, and your wife sent this over to you, sir. Here's the mail, too. The postmaster didn't want to give it to me, but Mr. Keeler told him it was all right, and that I belonged with the crew over here."

Unconsciously his tones were full of pride as he made this assertion, and the grocer had evidently done more to please the lad in making that assertion than he would ever know.

But Abner seemed to be staring down at something.

"Seems like as if yuh bed ben a leetle mite keerless, son, with them trousers. Don't strike me thet burn was on 'em yesterday," he remarked.

"It wasn't, Mr. Peake. I got that last night," he said, quickly.

"Doin' what?" went on Abner, who seemed to guess that there was a story back of it all that he ought to hear.

"Putting out the pigsty, that was on fire, sir."

"What's that? Who sot it afire, I'd like to know? Them pigs never has smoked, leastways not yit. Jest tell me the hull bloomin' thing, lad."

To begin at the start Darry had to take up the subject of his encounter on the road, and from that he went on until the whole story had been told, including the visit of Hank Squires.

CHAPTER IX: THE SIGNAL ROCKET

Abner Peake made no comment until the end had been reached.

Then he smote one hand into the palm of the other, and relieved his feelings in the expressive way one would expect a coast "cracker" to do.

"This sorter thing has got to stop! It's sure the limit wen them varmints set about burnin' a honest man's buildin's up! I'll take the law into my own hands onless somethin' is did soon. P'raps that parson kin manage to rouse up the village, and upset old Dilks. Ef so be it falls through I'm gwine to take a hand, no matter what happens."

He immediately told the whole story to his companions at the station, and they, of course, sympathized with him to a man.

"That Dilks gang has got to be run out of Ashley, root and branch, daddy and sons, for they're all alike," declared the keeper, Mr. Frazer, who was a man of considerable intelligence—indeed, no one could hold the position he did unless fairly educated and able to manage the various concerns connected with the station. "It's a burning shame that the families of men who are away from home in the service of the Government can't be left unmolested. I'm going to take the matter up with the authorities the next time the boat comes to this station."

The life savers asked Darry many questions, but he was careful not to fully commit himself with regard to identifying the three culprits.

"Course he couldn't say, boys. Don't forget Darry's new in this section, and most o' the boys is strangers to him. But he's put his trade-mark on one as won't forget it in a hurry. And for me I'd be willing to wager my week's pay that young Jim Dilks was leadin' them raiders in their rascally work," declared one of the crew, a stalwart young fellow named Sandy Monks.

By this time the storm began to break, and it became necessary for the keeper to make good use of his glass in the endeavor to place any vessel chancing to be within range, so that in case of trouble later in the night they would have some idea as to the character of the imperiled craft.

Darry watched everything that was done with eager eyes.

After an early supper, in which he participated with the men of the station, he saw the guard that had the first patrol don their storm clothes, and prepare to pass out to tramp the beach, exchanging checks when they met other members of the next patrol to prove that through the livelong night they had been alive to their duty.

Abner was on the second watch. He had consented to let the boy go out with him, and share his lonely tramp, for he seemed to realize that just then it was the most ardent wish in the heart of our hero to become a life saver like himself.

The rain came down in sheets, and the thunder rattled, while lightning played in strange fashion all around; but this storm was not in the same class with the dreadful West India hurricane that had sent the poor Falcon on to the cruel reefs, to wind up her voyaging forever.

Darry might have liked to sit up and listen to the men tell about former experiences; but the keeper chased them to their beds, knowing that it was necessary to secure some sleep, since they must remain up the latter half of the night.

A hand touching his face aroused Darry.

"Time to git up, lad, if so be yuh wants to go along," came a voice which he recognized as belonging to Abner, though he had been dreaming of the captain.

He was quickly dressed and out of doors.

It seemed to be still raining, and the wind howled worse than ever, though but little thunder accompanied the vivid flashes of lightning.

Having been giving some spare waterproof garments in the shape of oilskins, and a sou'wester, Darry felt himself prepared to face any conditions that might arise during his long walk with his friend.

Taking lantern and coster lights for signalling, Abner set out, another patrol going in the opposite direction.

Those who had been out for hours had returned to the station in an almost exhausted condition, and at the time Abner and Darry left they were warming up with a cup of coffee, strong spirits being absolutely forbidden while on duty.

Darry asked questions when the wind allowed of his speaking, which was not all the time, to be sure.

He wanted to know how the patrol learned when a ship was in distress, and Abner answered that sometimes they saw lights on the reefs; again the lightning betrayed the perilous condition of the recked vessel; but usually they learned of the need of assistance through rockets sent up by those on board, and which were answered by the coast guard.

Captain Harley had not been given a chance to send such an appeal for help, since he had been swept overboard just after the brigantine struck; besides, the vessel was a complete wreck at the time, and without a single stick in place could never have utilized the breeches buoy even had a line been shot out across her bows by means of the Lyle gun.

In two hours they had gone to the end of their route, and exchanged checks with the other patrol coming from the south. Then the return journey was begun.

Almost an hour had elapsed since turning back, and they were possibly more than half way to the station, when suddenly Darry, who chanced to be looking out to sea, discovered an ascending trail of fire that seemed to mount to the very clouds, when it broke, to show a flash of brilliant light.

"See!" he had exclaimed, dragging at the sleeve of his companion's coat, for Abner was plodding along steadily, as if his mind was made up to the effect that there was going to be no call for help on this night.

"A rocket! a signal!" cried the old life saver, at once alive to the occasion.

His first act was to unwrap one of the coster lights, and set it on fire.

This was intended to inform those on board the ship that their call for assistance had been seen, and that the lifeboat would soon be started if conditions allowed of its getting through the surf; for there are occasionally times when the sea runs so high that it proves beyond human endeavor to launch the boat.

Having thus done his duty, so far as he could, Abner set out on a run for the station, knowing that unless the full crew was on hand all efforts to send out the boat would be useless.

Darry kept at his heels, though he could have outrun the older man had he so desired, being sturdy and young.

Stumbling along, sometimes falling flat as they met with obstacles in the darkness, they finally came within sight of the lights of the station.

Here they found all excitement, for the signal rockets had of course been seen by the lookout, and all was in readiness to run the boat out of its shed.

Darry found that he could certainly make himself useful in giving a helping hand, and with a will the boat was hurried down to the edge of the water that rolled up on the beach.

All they waited for now was the coming of one man, whose beat happened to be a little longer than any other, but who should have shown up ere now.

As the minutes passed the anxiety of the helmsman grew apace, for those on the stranded vessel were sending more rockets up, as though they believed their peril to be very great.

The men stood at their places, ready to push at the word, and then leap aboard.

Darry was with them, eager and alert; indeed, he had done such good service up to now that the stout Mr. Frazer cast an eye toward him more than once, as though tempted to ask him to take the place of the missing man, who must have had an accident on the way, perhaps spraining an ankle over some unseen obstacle that came in his way as he ran headlong.

Darry saw him talking with Abner, who looked his way, and shook his head as if hardly willing to give his consent.

Just as his hopes ran high, and the words seemed trembling on the lips of the helmsman a shout was heard and the missing man came limping down to take his place without a complaint, though as it afterwards turned out he had a bad sprain.

Then the wild word was given, the men heaved, the surf boat ran into the water, with the men jumping aboard, oars flashed out on either side, and were dipped deep, after which the boat plunged into the next wave, rode on its crest like a duck, made a forward move, and then darkness shut it from the gaze of the lad left behind.

CHAPTER X: JIM THE BULLY

Although he could not accompany the life savers in the boat Darry had been given duties to perform, which he went about with a vim.

One of these was to keep the fire burning, so that it might serve as a beacon to the life savers as they toiled at the oars.

What with the darkness, and the flying spray that seemed almost as dense as fog, it was a difficult task to hold their bearings, and this glare upon the clouds overhead was essential.

By this time several other men arrived on the scene, having taken chances upon the bay when it was seen that the night would be stormy.

They were only too willing to assist, and as time passed many anxious looks were cast out upon the dashing sea in expectation of seeing the boat returning, possibly with some of the passengers or crew of the vessel in danger.

Finally a loud shout was heard:

"There they come!"

Upon the top of an incoming billow the lifeboat was seen perched, with the men laboring at the oars to keep it steady, and the steersman standing at his post, every muscle strained to hold the craft from broaching to.

It was a wild sight, and every nerve in Darry's body seemed to thrill as he kept his eyes glued upon that careening boat.

On it came, sweeping in with the wash of the agitated sea, until finally it was carried far up the beach, where men, rushing in waist deep, seized hold and prevented the undertow from dragging it out again.

Then the crew jumped out to lend their aid.

Darry saw that quite a number of strangers were aboard, who had undoubtedly been taken from the vessel.

They were passengers, the captain and crew refusing to abandon their craft.

The steamer being head on, was not in as bad a condition as might otherwise have been the case; and as the storm promised to be short-lived, the commander had decided to try and await the coming of tugs from the city to drag his vessel off.

The telephone to the mainland was immediately put to good use, and a message sent to a salvage company that would bring a couple of strong sea-going tugs to the scene inside of ten hours.

Abner had labored with the rest.

He was more or less tired when Darry found him, after the boat had been drawn up on the beach, but not housed, since it might be needed again; but this sort of thing was an old story in his life, and in comparison with some of his labors the adventure of the night had been rather tame.

In the morning Darry started across the bay again, homeward bound.

He was sorry to leave the beach, so much was his heart wrapped up in the work of the life savers.

The day was bright and fine after the short storm which had seemed to clear the air wonderfully.

He could see a few boats moving about, some of them oyster sloops or dredgers, other pleasure craft belonging to the rich sportsmen who had already commenced to drift down in pursuit of their regular fall shooting.

Occasionally the distant dull boom of a gun told that a few ducks were paying toll on their passage south.

Darry looked longingly at a splendid motor-boat that went swiftly past him.

The young fellow on board seemed to be having a most delightful time, and it was only natural for any boy to envy him.

It was noon when our hero arrived home. Mrs. Peake was interested in all he had to tell about the trip of the life savers.

"We get used to hearing these things," she said, "but all the same it keeps the wives of the life savers feeling anxious. Some night it happens one of the crew of the lifeboat goes out and does not return. At any time it may be my turn. I know three widows now."

"I think they ought to pick out the unmarried men," remarked Darry, who had himself been considering this very subject.

"They do, I believe, as far as they can; but we must have bread, and the number of available surfmen is small. But those who win their living from the sea learn to expect these things sooner or later. It is only a question of time."

After a bit of lunch Darry was sent to the village on an errand.

This was how he happened to see Jim Dilks again.

The meeting occurred just before Darry reached the grocer's, and as Jim was totally unaware of his coming he had no chance to assume airs.

Darry looked at him eagerly, as though expecting to make a discovery; and this anticipation met with no disappointment.

There could be no doubt about Jim limping, and once he instinctively put his hand back of him as if to rub a spot that pained more or less.

Darry understood what it meant, and that he had not sent that shower of fine bird shot after the trio of desperate young scamps in vain.

If Hank Squires wanted positive evidence as to who had been connected with the firing of Mrs. Peake's out-buildings he could find it upon an examination of the person of Jim Dilks.

When the good-for-nothing caught sight of Darry it was surprising how he stiffened up and walked as upright as a drum-major.

Darry had lost all respect for the prowess of the young ruffian, after that one trial of strength, when he had found Jim so lacking in everything that goes to make up a fighter. He had the feeling that he could snap his fingers in the other's face.

Being a boy he could not help from addressing the ex-bully, and rubbing it in a little, for Jim was scowling at him ferociously.

"Hello, Jim, how's the sprain—or was it rheumatism you had in your wrist? Sorry to see it's gone down now into one of your legs, and makes you limp. I tell you what's good for that sort of thing. First, be sure to take out any foreign substance, such as gravel, lead or anything like that; then wash it well and rub on some sort of ointment. Follow the directions and it will work fine," he said, as soberly as though he meant every word.

If anything, Jim scowled worse than before, since his guilty soul knew that this boy suspected his connection with the lawless act of the recent night.

"Saw yer comin' acrost the bay this mornin'; say, was yer over on ther beach with the life savers? Did a boat go ter pieces on the reefs?" he asked.

Darry saw that the other was swallowing his resentment in order to pick up information, and he remembered what dark stories he had heard in connection with the men who formed the companions of Jim's father—that they were termed wreckers, and some said they had reached a point of desperation where they did not hesitate to lure a vessel upon the reefs in order to profit from the goods that would float ashore after she went to pieces.

Possibly the older Dilks and his cronies may have been abroad on the preceding night, hovering around in hopes of a windfall; and Jim was eager to learn whether such a chance had come.

"Not last night, I'm glad to say. There was a steamer aground, but only the passengers would come ashore, the captain and crew remaining on board waiting for the tugs to arrive," replied Darry.

Jim's face fell several degrees.

He would have been satisfied to hear that a dozen poor sailors had been lost if it meant a big haul for the wreckers of the coast.

"Say, be yer goin' to stay 'round this district," asked the bully, changing the subject suddenly.

"Well, Mrs. Peake wants me to remain with her, and so does Abner. I'm thinking about it. When I make my mind up I'll let you know, Jim. If it's stay, why we can have it all over again. I want to warn you, Jim. You're going to get yourself into trouble if you keep on the way you're bent now. There's a law that sends a man to the penitentiary for setting fire to a neighbor's house," he said, as sternly as he could.

"Never set fire ter a house," declared Jim, quickly.

"Well, it doesn't matter whether it's a house or a barn or a hencoop. If Hank Squires could only find some positive evidence against you he says he'd lock you up right now; and Jim, I know how he could get all the evidence he needs."

"'Taint so," flashed out the bully, but looking alarmed all the same; while his hand half instinctively sought his rear.

"I think that an examination of those ragged trousers you wear would show where a few fine bird-shot peppered you as you ran. Perhaps both the other fellows got a touch of the same medicine, too, so you'd have company, Jim, when you went up."

"It's a lie. I never sot that pigpen on fire!"

"Oh! you know it was a pigpen, then, do you? I spoke of a chicken coop only."

"Heerd 'em torkin' about it. Thet ole busybody, Miss Pepper, she war in ther store wen I was gittin' somethin' fur mam, and she sed as how she'd run this village if she war a man, an' the feller as set fire ter a honest woman's pigpen 'd git his'n right peart. Like fun she wud," returned Jim, quickly.

"She's got her eye on you, Jim. She believes you led that gang. Going, eh, good-bye."

CHAPTER XI: A GLORIOUS PROSPECT

Jim had heard enough. He was beginning to be a bit afraid lest this sturdy new boy who had mastered him so easily in their late encounter, take a notion to investigate his condition physically; and there were several little punctures that just then Jim did not care to have seen.

Darry watched the bully saunter away, and it made him smile to see what an effort the other kept up his careless demeanor, when every step must have caused him more or less pain.

Perhaps Jim, in spite of his bombastic manner, might have received a lesson, and would be a little more careful after this how he acted.

So he walked to the store, completed his purchases, and was waiting for them to be tied up when who should enter but the young fellow he had seen in the beautiful cedar motor-boat out on the bay.

He was dressed like a sportsman, and there was a frank, genial air about him that quite attracted Darry.

Apparently he had dropped in to get his mail, for he walked over to the little cubby hole where a clerk sat.

As his eyes in roving around chanced to fall on Darry, and the latter saw him give a positive start, and he seemed to be staring at him as though more than casually interested.

Then he spoke to the clerk, who looked out toward Darry and apparently went on to explain that he was a stranger in the community, having been on a brigantine recently wrecked on the deadly reefs off the shore.

The young man sauntered around until Darry left.

Just as our hero put the last of the small shanties that formed the outskirts of Ashley behind him he caught the sound of hurrying steps.

Thinking of Jim and his ugly promise of future trouble he half turned, but to his surprise and pleasure he saw that it was the owner of the launch, and that apparently the youth was hurrying to overtake him.

What his curiosity was founded on Darry could not say; but presumed the other had liked his looks and wanted to strike up an acquaintance.

It would not be the first time such a thing had happened to him.

"Good morning, or rather good afternoon," said the stranger. "I believe they told me your name was Darry, and that you are stopping with one of the life savers. My name is Paul Singleton, and I'm down here, partly for my health, and also to enjoy the shooting. It turns out to be pretty lonely work, and I'm looking for a congenial companion to keep me company and help with the decoys later. I'm willing to pay anything reasonable, and I carry enough grub for half a dozen. My boat is small, but affords ample sleeping accommodations for two. How would you like to try it," and the youth smiled broadly.

Darry was thrilled at the prospect, although he could not see his way clear to accept it just then.

First of all he would not think of doing so without consulting Abner, who had been so kind, and who expected him to remain with the little family; then, it was nice to believe that Mrs.

Peake would feel sorry to lose him; and last of all he knew little or nothing about the bay or the ways of guides, and the duties connected with the profession.

"I'd like it first-rate, but just now I don't see how I could accept," he replied.

"If it's a question of wages—" began the young man, who was watching the various expressions flit over Darry's face with an eager eye.

"Not at all. I was only thinking of my duty to Abner Peake and his wife, who have been so good to me. Perhaps later on I might accept, providing you have not already filled the place."

"I suppose you know best, but somehow I've taken a notion I'd like to have you along with me, Darry. For a week or two I mean to just knock around here, sometimes ashore and again afloat. Perhaps when the shooting begins in earnest you may be able to give me a different answer."

"At any rate by that time I shall know more about the bay and the habits of the ducks that drop in here. I'm a stranger, you see, Mr. Singleton, and though I've done some hunting in India and other places where our ship lay at anchor for weeks, I know little about this sport. I can cook as well as the next fellow, and of course know something about boats, though more used to sails than gasoline."

"You're too modest, Darry. Some chaps would have jumped at the chance to have a fine time. But I like you all the better for it. I see you are in a hurry, so I won't detain you any longer. It's understood then that if you can get off later you'll come to me?"

"I'll only be too glad to do so, Mr. Singleton," was Darry's answer.

The young fellow thrust out his hand, while his gaze still remained riveted on Darry's face.

As the boy walked rapidly away, feeling a sense of overpowering delight at the prospect ahead if all things went well, something caused him to glance back, and he saw Paul Singleton shaking his head while sauntering toward the village, as if something puzzled him greatly.

Darry could not understand what ailed the other, or how anything about his appearance should attract so fine a young gentleman.

He told Mrs. Peake about it, and while she looked displeased at first, Darry was so apparently loth to leave her that the better element in the woman's nature soon pushed to the front.

"Of course you can go, after a little. There's nothing to prevent. It will be a fine thing for you, and may lead to something better. We have put through one winter without a man in the house, and can again. Time was when all my children were little, and even then Abner used to be away most of the time. Don't worry about us, Darry. When the time comes, I say, go," was what she remarked.

How the skies were brightening for him!

And only a few days back he had faced such a gloomy prospect that it appalled him!

Now he whistled as he worked, rubbing up the various traps taken from Joe's box, and preparing to sally out for his first experience in trying to catch the muskrats that haunted the borders of the watercourses in the marshes near by.

Carrying that invaluable little notebook along for reference in case he should become puzzled about anything, and with a few traps slung over his shoulder Darry followed the paths along the edge of the marsh until he reached one that seemed to enter the waste land.

Joe had designated this as his favorite tramp, since it paralleled the creek, and the burrows of the little fur-bearing animals could be easily located.

Presently Darry was busily engaged in examining the bank, and it was not long before he had found what he sought.

This was a hole just below the water line.

There were also the tracks of the occupants close by, showing just how they issued from their snug home to forage for food.

He carefully set his trap under a few inches of water, so that the first rat coming forth and starting to climb the bank would set his hind feet in it.

The chain he fastened to a stake out in the creek.

This was done in order that the little rodent would be quickly drowned.

Trappers invariably follow this rule when after water animals, and it is not always through a spirit of mercy toward the victim that actuates their motive, but the fact that they would otherwise lose many a catch, since the captive in despair over its inability to escape would gnaw its foot off.

Having finished with the trap, Darry walked further into the marsh. It was a lonely place, seldom visited save by a few hunters in the season, who looked for mallard ducks there; or it might be some boy trapper, endeavoring to make a few dollars by catching some of the shy denizens wearing marketable fur coats.

Here a brace of snipe went spinning away, and a little further a blue crane got up and flapped off, his long legs sticking out like fishing poles.

In an hour or so the boy had placed all his traps. He had followed Joe's directions to the letter, and the morning would show as to whether he was to make a success of the venture.

One thing was positive, and it was this, that even should he find nothing in the traps he did not mean to give up; if he had made a mistake, then it must be rectified, even if he had to secure some old boat in order to carry out his operations without leaving a scent behind to alarm the game.

It was late in the afternoon when he reached home.

The twins ran to meet him as though already they looked upon him in the light of a member of the little family.

Darry threw first one and then the other up into the air, while they shrieked with laughter, and he could see that Mrs. Peake was looking on approvingly, as if her desolated mother heart was warming toward this lad who had never known what it was to have any one love him.

He had been thinking much that afternoon of Paul Singleton, even repeating the name of the young man over and over, as though striving to remember whether he could have ever heard it before, which did not seem likely.

And it was not so much anticipation of the good times coming that engaged his thought as that queer look on the face of Paul while they had been talking.

What could it mean?

CHAPTER XII: THE STOLEN TRAPS

In the morning Darry occupied himself repairing the damage done by the fire.

After he had done all the chores, even to assisting Mrs. Peake wash the breakfast dishes, and there seemed nothing else to be undertaken, he took Joe's shotgun on his shoulder and walked toward the marsh.

The woman, seeing how much he looked like her lost boy with the gun and the clothes, had a good cry when left to herself; but Darry did not know this.

As he approached his first trap he found himself fairly tingling with eagerness.

This was not because of the value involved in the skin of a muskrat, though it seemed as though each year the price was soaring as furs became more scarce; but he wanted to feel that he had learned his lesson well, and followed out the instructions given in Joe's little handbook.

The trap was gone!

He saw this with the first glance he cast over the low bank.

Did it have a victim in its jaws or had some marauder stolen it?

With a stick he groped in the deeper water, and catching something in the crotch he presently drew ashore the trap.

He had caught his first prize.

Of course he understood that when compared with the mink and the fox, a muskrat is an ignorant little beast at best, and easily captured; but for a beginning it was worth feeling proud over.

Setting the trap again in the hope that there might be others in the burrow, one of which would set his foot in trouble on the succeeding night, Darry went on.

He found only one more victim to the half dozen traps.

Perhaps he had been too careless with the others and left plain traces of his presence that had warned the cunning rodents.

Having placed all his traps in the water again, he started back home, swinging the two "muskies" in one hand, while carrying his gun in the other.

After leaving the marsh he chanced to look back and was surprised to see a boy come out and start on a run toward the village.

Darry had very little acquaintance with the village lads, and could not make up his mind whether he had ever seen this fellow before or not; but once or twice he thought he detected evidence of a limp in his gait when he fell into a walk, and this brought to mind Jim and his two cronies.

It was not Jim, but at the same time there was no reason why it should not be one of his bodyguard, "the fellows who sneezed when Jim took snuff," as Mrs. Peake had said in speaking of the lot.

Suppose this did happen to be Sim Clark or Bowser, what had he been doing in the marsh?

Could it be possible that the fellow had been spying on him, and was now hastening to report to his chief?

They might think to annoy him by stealing the traps he had placed, or at least robbing them of any game.

Darry shut his teeth hard at the idea.

He made up his mind that he would go out earlier on the following day, even if, in order to do so, he had to get up long before daylight to accomplish his various chores.

No doubt he made rather a sorry mess of the job when he came to removing those first pelts—at least it took him half a dozen times as long as a more experienced trapper would have needed in order to accomplish the task.

Still, when he finally had them fastened to a couple of boards left by Joe, he felt that he had reason to be satisfied with his first attempt.

Mrs. Peake declared they seemed to look all right, and as each represented a cash money value of some forty or fifty cents, Darry realized that there was a little gold mine awaiting him in that swamp, providing those miserable followers of Jim allowed him to work it.

Several times he awoke during the night and started up, thinking he heard suspicious sounds again, but they proved false alarms.

He was glad to see the first peep of day, and quickly tumbled out to set about his various duties of starting the fire, bringing in water and wood, and later on chopping a supply of fuel sufficient to last through the day.

When Mrs. Peake gave him permission to go Darry hurried off.

Again he carried the gun, thinking he might find a chance to bag a fine fat duck or two, which Mrs. Peake declared she would be glad to have for dinner.

Arriving at the scene of his first triumph of the previous day, he discovered once more that the trap was gone from the bank.

Again he fished for it with the crotched stick, but despite his efforts there was no trap forthcoming.

Finally, filled with a sudden suspicion, he crawled down to examine the stake in the water to which the chain had been secured.

The stake was there all right but no trap rewarded his search.

With his heart beating doubly fast, Darry sped along the path to where he had located his second trap, only to find it also missing.

Now he knew that it could be no accident, but a base plot to upset all his calculations and deprive him of the fruits of his industry.

The thing that angered him most of all was the fact that he must face Mrs. Peake and tell her he had lost the treasures she valued so highly.

He shut his teeth together firmly.

"They won't keep them, not if I know it," he muttered. "I'll find out where they hide them. I'll get 'em again, sure as I live!"

The thieves had apparently done their evil work well. Not a single trap did he find in the various places where he had left them.

But one thing he saw that gave him a savage satisfaction, and this was the fact that there were footprints around the last one, in which the muddy water had not yet had time to become clear.

Darry believed from this that those who had rifled his belongings could not have left the scene more than a few minutes.

Perhaps if he were smart he could overtake them and demand restitution.

It stood to reason that the rascals could not have returned along the same path, for he would have met them.

He bent down to examine the ground and could easily see where the marks of several wet and heavy shoes continued along the trial that followed the creek.

Darry immediately started off on a run.

Hardly five minutes later, as he turned a bend, he had a glimpse of a figure just leaving the path and entering the woods bordering the swamp.

So far as he knew he had not been noticed; but to make sure he crept along under the shelter of neighboring bushes until he reached the place where the moving figure had caught his eye.

Voices now came to his ear, and it was easy enough to follow the three slouching figures that kept pushing deeper into the swamp.

He even saw his precious traps on their backs, together with several muskrats which Jim himself carried.

Perhaps their first idea was to throw the traps into the oozy water of the swamp, so that they could never be found again; but then those steel contraptions represented a cash value of a dollar or so, and money appealed strongly to these fellows; so they hung on, with the idea of placing them in a hollow tree, where, later, they could be found and sold.

Darry knew that he was going to recover his own, and he now watched the movements of the three with more or less curiosity.

All the while he kept drawing nearer, fearful lest they discover him before he could get close enough to hold them up; for should they run in different directions he could not expect to accomplish his end.

Then he saw what brought them to this place.

A rude shack made of stray boards, and branches from trees loomed up.

It was evidently a secret hide-out of the gang, where they came when matters got too warm either at home or among the neighbors whose hen roosts they had been pillaging.

When Darry saw Jim throw his bunch of game on the ground, he knew his chase was at an end, and that presently, when he felt good and ready, he could turn the tables on his enemies.

Lying there watching them start a fire and prepare to cook something they had brought along, he even chuckled to imagine how surprised the trio of young rascals would be when he popped up like a jack-in-the-box.

CHAPTER XIII: JOE'S SHOTGUN SECURES A SUPPER

One of the fellows with Jim, and whom he addressed as Sim, gathered the six stolen traps together and held them up laughingly.

"A bully find, fellers; but if I had me way I'd let 'em lie and snooped the musky out every day. Why it'd be like takin' candy from the baby, that's what. But Jim there wanted to kerry off the hull bunch," he said, swinging the traps idly to and fro.

"I wanted ter let him know I allers kep' me word. When he finds 'em gone I bet yer he knows who's had a hand in it; but he caint prove nothin'. I kin snap me fingers in his face, an' tell him ter chase hisself. Here, Bowser, git that fire goin' in a hurry. I'm pretty near starved. The ole man chased me outen the house last night, an' ther ole woman won't give me a bite. Reckon I'll hev ter hustle fur meself arter this. Dad's as mad as hops 'cause he aint hed a chanct ter pick up any stuff on the beach fur three moons. If it keeps on, him and his gang 'll hev ter do sumpin different ter make biz good."

Darry did not care to linger any longer.

He wanted those traps and the animals that had been taken from them, and he meant to have them.

"Why, hello, boys!"

The three young rascals sprang erect when they heard these words, and their amazement can be imagined at discovering the object of their recent raid standing there not twenty feet away, holding Joe Peake's old shotgun carelessly in his hands.

In that moment the real nature of each of them showed itself—Sim Clark darted into cover and ran away at the top of his speed like the coward he was, Bowser fell on his knees and wrung his hands, being weak when it came to a showdown; but Jim Dilks, ruffian as he was, scorned to do either, and stood his ground, like a wolf brought to bay and showing its fangs.

"I see you have been so kind as to gather a few traps of mine together. And as I live if you haven't relieved me of the trouble of fishing for several rats. Very kind of you, Jim. Now, don't say a word, and just keep where you are, or by accident something might happen. Guess you know what shot feels like when it hits. Once ought to be enough, and this time you're so close it might be serious. Now, listen to me, once and for all, Jim Dilks, and you Bowser, I'm going right back and set these traps where I think I'll find more game. You touch a finger to one of them at your peril. I'll let Hank Squires know all about this shack here, and what you've been up to. The first trap that is missing means the whole three of you behind the bars. That's all."

Jim never opened his mouth. He was awed for the time being, and watched Darry pick up the traps, together with the three muskrats, swing the lot over his shoulder and walk away.

The boy did not know but what they might attempt to jump upon him yet and kept on the alert; but when he presently looked back upon hearing a shout, he found that Jim was only relieving his wounded feelings by kicking the kneeling Bowser vigorously.

Darry did just as he had said he would.

He went a little further into the marsh, thinking that since so many feet had been trampling around the bank of the creek the game might have become shy; but he set the six traps, and even marked the tree nearest each, so that the location could be easily found by himself or others, inclined that way.

Such bold tactics would do more to keep Jim and his set from disturbing the traps than the utmost secrecy.

When Darry went back home, he thought it best not to say anything about his adventure to Mrs. Peake; but having occasion to go to the village later in the day he sought out the constable, whom he found cleaning up his garden patch and burning the refuse.

Old Hank amused him. The fellow was always indulging in mysterious hints as to what he was going to do some day soon, and doubtless his intentions were all right, but, as Miss Pepper had truly said, he lacked the backbone to carry them out.

Old Jim Dilks and his crew of trouble breeders had dominated the vicinity so long now that it was hard to break away from their sway.

The officer of the law was in his shirt sleeves, so that his fine nickel badge could not shine upon his manly breast; but as he saw Darry approach, and scented coming business, he drew his tall figure up as if in that way he could at least represent the majesty of the law.

Hank had an idea that he possessed an eye that was a terror to evil-doers, when to tell the truth his gaze was as mild and peaceful as that of a babe.

"Glad to see you, Darry. Hope there ain't been any more doings up at your place? I'm laying for the slippery rascals, and hope to have them dead to rights soon; but you know men in my profession have to go slow. A mistake is a serious thing in the eye of the law," he said, offering his hand in a friendly fashion.

"There's nothing wrong up at the house, sir; but I wanted to tell you something I think you ought to know, in case the time comes when you might want to find Jim Dilks and his gang and they were not at home," began Darry.

The constable quailed a trifle, then grew stern.

"Big Jim or little Jim, which?" he said, anxiously.

"The boy who has tried to make things so warm for me. He and his crowd have a shack in the swamp, where they camp out from time to time. That's where you'll find them when wanted."

"Sure that's interesting news, lad. Can you tell me just where to look?"

He heaved a sigh of relief—then there was not any need of immediate haste, and Hank was a true Southern "cracker," always ready to postpone action.

"Leave the path along the creek just where it makes that sharp bend. A fallen tree marks the spot. Head due south until you sight a big live oak, the only one I noticed. The shack lies under its spreading branches, Mr. Squires. I thought you ought to know. Besides, I told Jim and his crowd I meant to inform you."

"What! you saw Jim there, and his crowd with him? I wonder they let you get out of the swamp without a beating," exclaimed the constable, surprised, and looking at this newcomer as though he could hardly believe his senses.

"They knew better. The fact is, sir, I had a shotgun with me. Perhaps they may have had a recent experience with such a little tool. But no matter, they let me gather up my traps and the three muskrats taken from them, and never offered to put out a hand to stop me."

"Traps—muskrats—look here, now I begin to see light, and can give a guess how it came you were there in that swamp. You followed the rascals there."

"To tell the truth, I did, for I was determined to get back what they had taken."

"Bully for you, lad. If you had dropped in on us some time back we might have had a different class of boys around here by now. You're a reformer, that's what you are. First you knocks that tyrant Jim down; then you pepper him with shot after he has fired the pigpen of your new home, and now you brave him in his own dooryard. That's reforming all right, and I hope you keep at it until you've reformed the ugly beggar into the penitentiary. I begin to pluck up hope that soon public spirit will be so aroused that we can do something right. Would you mind shaking hands with me again, Darry. It does me good, sure it does."

Of course Darry complied, though he had his doubts as to whether Mr. Squires would ever have the nerve to connect himself with any movement looking to the purging of Ashley village of its rough element.

In fact, if anything were ever done he believed such women as Miss Pepper would be the ones to run the evil-doers out of town, and put up the bars.

Darry had taken the three animals home, pleased to know that after all half his traps had found victims on this second day.

He judged from this that he was doing very well, and with a little more experience could consider himself a full-fledged trapper.

Later in the afternoon he thought of the ducks, and passing out upon the marsh walked until he discovered several feeding among the wild rice, when he started to creep up on them with infinite cunning.

Reaching at last a bunch of grass as near as he could hope to go he waited until two were close together, when he fired his right barrel.

As the remaining mallard started to rise in a clumsy fashion Darry gave him the benefit of the other barrel.

When Mrs. Peake saw what fine birds he had secured she was loud in her praise, for their coming meant at least one good meal without cost, and every cent counted in this little family.

Again Darry busied himself with his pelts.

He was pleased to find how much easier the job seemed after his experience of the preceding day; and when the skins had been stretched upon the boards they had a cleaner look that satisfied the eye.

After that he plucked the three ducks for the good woman, saving her a task she never fancied, and winning her thanks.

Then he looked after the gun, believing that it is wise to always keep such a weapon in the best of order, since it serves its owner faithfully when called upon.

"I had some visitors while you were away," announced Mrs. Peake, when after supper they were seated by the table.

Darry looked up from his work of whittling more stretching boards, interested at once.

CHAPTER XIV: THE LONELY VIGIL OF THE COAST PATROL

Mrs. Peake looked amused.

"A young man called on me," she said.

Dairy's face lighted up.

"It must have been Mr. Singleton!" he exclaimed, eagerly.

She nodded in the affirmative.

"Did he come to see me?" he asked.

"No, I rather think he wanted to have a little talk with me. You see he guessed from what you told him that it all was because of me you wouldn't go with him, and he just dropped in, he said, to have a neighborly chat, and let me know how much he was interested in a boy by the name of Darry."

"That was fine of him. What did you think, wasn't he all I said?"

"As nice a young gentleman as I ever met. He asked a lot of questions about you."

"Of course. He had a right to. When a gentleman asks a strange fellow to go off with him on a cruise it's only business for him to learn all he can about whether the other is honest and all that. You told him I never touched liquor, I hope?"

"He never asked about such things. In fact, it was all in connection with your past he seemed interested."

"My past—how could he be interested in that? He never saw me before." Yet, strange to say, the fact seemed to thrill Darry through and through; for he was still hugging that hope to his heart, and wondering if some day he might not be lucky enough to learn who and what he was.

"Well, all I can say is that he kept asking me all about you came here, why you were Darry, and what your other name might be; when he learned that you never knew who your parents were he seemed to be strangely agitated. He didn't take me into his confidence; but I'm morally convinced that Mr. Singleton believes he is on the track of some sort of discovery. I heard him ask Miss Pepper, who was hurrying over, seeing I had a visitor, if there was a telegraph office in Ashley; and when he left he was saying to himself: 'I must let her know—this may be important.' It would be a fine thing for you, my boy, if circumstances brought you face to face with some rich relative so soon after you landed on the soil of America."

Darry drew a long breath, and shook his head.

"It would be great, as you say, whether my father or mother were rich or poor, it wouldn't matter a bit to me; but I'm afraid you're getting too far along. Perhaps what you heard him say may refer to another affair entirely. No matter, I like Mr. Singleton, and have from the start. If we go off together I know I'd enjoy it first-rate in that dandy little motor-boat of his. I haven't said I would for sure. I mean to wait a while and see how things come out here ashore."

She knew he was thinking of Jim Dilks and his scheming for mischief—that he believed the fact of her giving him shelter and a home had drawn upon her head the vindictive fury of the lawless rascal, who, finding the little home undefended if Darry went away, might think it safe to continue his persecution.

When Darry strode forth into the marsh the next day he again carried the gun.

He found his traps all safe. Undoubtedly his defiance had had its effect upon the mind of Jim; and however much he may have felt like repeating the thievish act which Darry's prompt arrival on the scene had nipped in the bud, he dared not attempt it.

He was beginning to be afraid of this young chap who kept a chip on his shoulder, and dared him to knock it off.

This time four victims attested to the skill with which the new trapper attended to his business.

Already was the list reaching respectable proportions.

He expected to cross over that afternoon to see Abner, and carry the mail again; and it would be with satisfaction that he could inform his good friend how the traps Joe had left behind were still fulfilling their destiny at the same old stand.

The sky was clouded over when he started out on his long trip.

He had during his leisure minutes fashioned a sort of sail that could be used with the wind astern; and as this happened to be the case now Darry got it in position for service.

With the sail, he just rushed along over the bay; and all the while sat there taking his ease instead of dragging at the oars.

Having spent some years on the waters there was little in connection with boats, big or little, that the lad did not know.

He had found some good wood which Abner had expected to use for the purpose at some future date, and one oar was already pretty well advanced.

By the time he crossed again he believed he would have them both completed; and at that they would be nothing of which anyone need feel ashamed.

The favoring wind kept up until he drew in to the little landing where, as before, Abner stood waiting for him.

That was a great night for Darry. First there came the supper with those jolly fellows, whose laughter and jokes he enjoyed so much; after that a nice quiet chat with Abner, who asked for all the news, and was deeply interested in his success in catching the sly denizens of the marsh; although he frequently sighed while Darry was speaking, and the boy could easily comprehend that at such times the poor man was picturing in his mind how Joe used to go through with the same experiences.

When Darry thought it only right to tell how the three cronies had stolen his possessions, and how he had recovered them, Abner slapped his hand down on his knee, and exclaimed:

"I reckon Mr. Fraser was right t'other day when he sez as how the sun o' the Dilks tribe began to set when yuh kim ashore from that wreck. Somehow yuh seem to be hittin' 'em hard, son. I aint much o' a prophet, sence I caint even tell wot the weather's gwine to be tomorry; but I seem to just know from the way things is a heapin' up that they's gwine to be a big heave soon, an' that means the Dilks has got to move on—Ashley don't want ther kind no more."

Darry insisted on accompanying Abner when it came his turn to go out on his long patrol; this time it was in the earlier part of the night, so neither man nor boy thought of going to bed.

The night was not wholly dark, for there was a moon behind the clouds; but beyond a certain limited distance of the sea lay in gloom, only the steady wash of the incoming waves telling of the vast reach of water lying along toward the east.

They talked of many things as they plodded along the sandy beach.

Darry spoke for the first time of Paul Singleton, and his desire that he accompany him later on in his cruising up and down the series of connected bays that stretched for some hundreds of miles back of the sandbars.

Abner was silent at first, and the boy realized that he felt grieved to know there might come a break in the pleasant relations that had been established at home.

"Course it's only right yuh should accept, lad," he said presently, "It's give me much comfort to know yuh was gittin' on so well with the ole woman, for I've felt bad on 'count o' her many times sense he war taken. But it's a chance thet may never kim again, an' we cudn't 'spect to tie yuh down. Anyhow, your comin' hez been a good thing fur Nancy, an' I reckons she'll begin to perk up from now on. 'Sides, who knows wot may kim outen this? Jest as she sez thet younker aint interested in yuh jest acause he wants a feller in the boat along with him—I tell yuh he thinks he knows who yuh belong to, and that's a fack, son."

"Oh! I hope so; but I don't dare dream of it. But I'm glad you think well of his offer. I can earn some money that will help out at home, besides having a good time," said Darry, eagerly; though truth to tell, it was the faint hope lodged in his heart that he might learn something concerning his past that chief of all influenced him in his desire to go with the owner of the motor-boat.

"Glad to hear yuh say that word 'home,' boy. I hopes it is a home to yuh, an' allers will be. I've ben thinkin' that your comin' war the greatest favor Heaven ever sent to me an' mine. If it gives Nancy new life that means a lot to me."

Darry knew not what to say to this, but he found the rough hand of Abner, and with a hearty squeeze expressed his feelings far better than any words could ever have done.

CHAPTER XV: THE POWER OF MUSIC

It seemed as though luck favored Darry on this trip, for the wind veered around during the night, and blew out of the southeast when he was ready to start on his return voyage to the mainland.

Thus he was able to use his little sail to advantage both ways.

It was coming so hard off the ocean, however, that at the advice of Abner he took a reef in the canvas before leaving—the life saver had become so attached to his new boy by this time that he could not bear to see him taking any unnecessary chances on that sheet of treacherous water that had already deprived him of one son.

Darry was glad he had taken his friend's advice before half way across. Where the wind had a full sweep of the bay the waves were quite heavy, and it required all his skill as a sailor to keep his cranky little craft head on.

As it was, he reached his haven with a rush, and his tactics in making a landing aroused the admiration of several old fisherman who were lounging at the dock.

He had only time to accomplish several little messages at the store and get on the road for home when it began to drizzle.

Darry was sorry for this, for he had laid out to visit his traps again during the afternoon, not wishing to leave any game that may have been taken, too long in the water.

When later on at lunch he mentioned this to Mrs. Peake she said he would find an old oilskin jacket of Abner's behind the closet door in the hall, which Joe had been wont to don under similar circumstances.

So after all, he went forth, defying the elements, as a true sailor lad always does; and was rewarded for his labor by taking three more trophies from the firm-jawed traps.

Really it was beginning to look like business, with so many on the stretching boards; and Mrs. Peake smiled to see how careful the boy was in everything he undertook.

It spoke well for his future, if he carried the same principle into his whole life.

Of course Darry knew full well that the skins he was taking thus early in the fall were not as good in quality, and would not be apt to bring as high prices in the fur marts as those to be captured when real cold weather had set in; but there are times when one has to make hay while the sun shines; and he could not be sure that he would have the opportunity to do these things later.

Besides, the supply of rats seemed unlimited, so rapidly do they breed all over the Eastern coast, from Maine to the Florida line.

The rain continued all that night and the better part of the following day.

It was one of those easterly storms that generally last out portions of three days, and are followed by a lengthy spell of good weather, with touches of frost in the early mornings.

Darry made his regular pilgrimage to the marsh in spite of the rain, and this time found only two prizes to reward his diligence.

From this he determined that it was time to make a change of base, and set his traps in other places where the game might not be so wary.

At any rate he was having no further trouble with the Dilks crowd, and in that he found more or less satisfaction.

Unconscious of the fact that he was being watched from time to time by one of the cronies of which Jim boasted, Darry went about his business, satisfied to do his daily duties, and each night count some progress made.

Twice had he crossed the bay to the strip of sandy beach where the tides of the mighty Atlantic pounded unceasingly, day and night.

His coming was always eagerly anticipated by the whole crew of the life-saving station, and for a good reason.

It happened that on his visit just after the easterly storm had blown out, while they were all gathered around just before dark, chatting and joking, Darry cocked up his ear at the tweeking sound of a fiddle, which one of the men had drawn out of its case, and was endeavoring to play.

Altogether he made a most doleful series of sounds, which upon analysis might prove to be an attempt to play "Annie Laurie," though one would need all his wits about him to settle whether this were the tune, or "Home, Sweet Home."

The men looked daggers at the player, for the screeching sounds were certainly anything but pleasant.

Darry sauntered over. He had played since a little lad, some Italian having first taught him; and on the brigantine Captain Harley had a violin of more than ordinary make, with which he had coaxed the cabin boy to make melody by the hour.

"Sounds like a pretty good instrument?" suggested Darry to the would-be performer.

"They tell me that, boy; but you see I ain't much of a judge. P'raps in time I may get on to the racket, that is if the boys don't fire me and the fiddle out before-hand," replied the surfman, grinning, for his clumsy hands were really never intended by Nature to handle a violin bow.

"Would you mind letting me try it? I used to play a little."

At the first sound of that bow crossing the strings, after Darry had properly tuned the instrument every man sat up and took notice; and as the boy bent down and lovingly drew the sweetest chords from the violin that they had ever heard, they actually held their breath.

After that he was kept busy; indeed they would hardly let him have any rest, and that was why those rough men looked forward eagerly to the expected coming of Abner Peake's new boy.

It seemed as though he must know everything there was, and the music would turn from riotous ragtime to the most tender chords, capable of drawing tears from those eyes so unused to weeping.

It was a rare treat to Darry, too, for he dearly loved music, and the absence of his fiddle had made a gap in his life.

The month was now passing, and closer drew the stormy period when, with the advent of grim November, the duties of the beach patrol naturally grow more and more laborious, since there are greater possibilities of wrecks, with the strong winds and the fogs that bewilder mariners, and allow them to run upon the reefs when they believe they are scores of miles away from the danger zone.

The boom of guns could now be heard all day, and frequently Darry saw Northern sportsmen in the village; though as a rule they kept on board their yachts or else stayed at the various private clubs up or down the sound.

Jim Dilks and his gang still lay low. They awaited a favorable opportunity to carry out some evil scheme, whereby the boy they had come to fear, as well as hate, might be injured.

Well, they knew that he made daily trips into the marsh, and it would seem that they might find the chance they craved at such times; but there was one thing to deter them, and this was the fact that Darry never went to examine his traps without carrying that steady-shooting old shotgun.

The burnt child dreads the fire, and Jim had hardly ceased to rub his injured parts, so that the possibility of getting a second dose was not at all alluring in his eyes.

He was a good waiter, and he felt that sooner or later fortune would turn the trick for him, and the chance arise whereby he might pay back the debt he owed the "interloper," as he chose to deem Darry.

CHAPTER XVI: DARRY MEETS WITH A REBUFF

During these weeks Darry had accomplished many little jobs around his new home, things that had been wanting looking after for a long time; for Abner's visits were so few and far between that he had little time to mend broken doors, or put up shelves where they would save the "missus" steps.

If he went off with Paul Singleton later he would have no chance to look after these things, and so he made good use of his opportunities.

He had not seen the young gentleman once since, and upon making inquiries of the storekeeper, learned that he had gone to a very exclusive club to spend some little time.

Darry wondered whether he had been utterly forgotten.

Perhaps the youth had regretted asking him to keep him company; it may have been done on the spur of the moment, simply because he chanced to resemble someone he knew.

Once in the comfortable club, with experienced guides to attend him, and the very best points for shooting reserved, doubtless Paul Singleton had forgotten that there was such a boy as Darry in existence.

So he tried to forget about it, and make up his mind that he could find plenty of congenial work looking after his traps and assisting Abner's wife during the winter, with occasional trips across the sound, and possibly a chance to pull an oar in the surfboat, should luck favor him.

All this while he had taken toll of the feathered frequenters of the marsh, and many a plump fowl graced the table of the Peake family, thanks to the faithful old gun, and the steady nerves back of it.

Darry soon learned where there were squirrels to be found, and twice he had brought in a mess of the gray nutcrackers, though not so fond of hunting them as other game.

And one day he had delighted the good housewife with four nice quail, or as they were known in this section, "pa'tridge," which he had dropped out of a bevy that got up before him in the brush close to the woods where he looked for squirrel.

He knew that something had been troubling Mrs. Peake, but it was a long time before he could tempt her to speak of it.

It concerned money matters, of course, as is nearly always the case when trouble visits the poor.

Abner had been incautious enough to put a little mortgage upon his humble home in order to help a relative who was in deep distress because of several sudden deaths in her family.

He should not have done it, to be sure, but Abner had a big heart, as Darry well knew, and simply could not resist the pleading of his cousin.

No doubt she meant well, but circumstances had arisen that prevented her from repaying the debt, and for the want of just one hundred dollars the Peakes were in danger of being dispossessed.

Of course the mortgage was in the hands of a money shark, for even little villages boast their loan offices, where some usurer expects to get ten per cent. on his money, and will not hesitate to foreclose if it is not forthcoming.

Abner's friends were all as poor as he was, and besides, he was so bashful about such things that he could never muster enough courage to mention his financial troubles to anybody.

When by degrees Darry managed to draw this story from Mrs. Peake he thought it all over while off on one of his swamp trips, and reached a conclusion.

That very day he stepped into the store of a man who as he chanced to know purchased the few furs that were taken in a season around that section.

He learned that pelts were bringing unusually good prices, and the party quoted as high as eighty cents for fall muskrat skins, properly treated.

When he got home, Darry counted his catch and found that he had some twenty-six in stock; with these he went back to the dealer, and struck a bargain whereby he came away with fourteen dollars in his pocket.

Then he made for the office of the lawyer who held the mortgage, thinking he could pay up the arrears of interest, and bring happiness to the face of his kind benefactress.

Just there he struck a snag.

The loan shark refused to accept the money.

He claimed that since they had defaulted on the interest the entire amount was due, and that he meant to have it, or foreclose.

Darry knew little of law, but he saw that Darius Quarles meant business, and suspected that for some reason he meant to hold to his advantage and give Abner Peake more or less trouble.

"Mr. Quarles, if you would only accept this interest now, I think I can promise that the whole sum will be paid by spring," Darry said, eagerly.

This was, of course, just what the lawyer did not want. He pretended to look skeptical, and shook his head.

"I suppose you are the boy Peake has adopted. Where did you get this money, may I ask? Did Nancy send you here with it?" he went on; and from the look in his cold, blue eyes, it was apparent that he would have enjoyed having the woman on her knees before him.

Darius Quarles was a very small-minded man evidently; even a boy like Darry could understand that.

"No, she does not know I have come here," replied our hero.

"Then where did you get the money? Boys as a rule don't sport such sums as fourteen dollars in a bunch. I haven't heard of any bank being robbed, or a sportsman being held up; but you understand, it looks suspicious, boy."

Darry flushed with mortification at the insult; but because of Mrs. Peake he managed to bite his lips and refrain from telling the curmudgeon just what he thought of him.

"I received that fourteen dollars not ten minutes ago from a merchant in this village. He will vouch for it if you ask him," he said, quietly, though his eyes flashed fire.

"Just mention his name, if you please. I might take a notion to drop in and see if he corroborates your assertion. As I am a magistrate as well as a lawyer, it is my bounden duty to make sure there is nothing crooked in such transactions as come under my observation. Who is the man?"

He tried to look stern, but the attempt was a failure. Nature had made Mr. Quarles only to appear small and mean.

"It was Mr. Ketcham, the hardware man," the boy answered.

"And what would he be paying you this munificent sum for? So far as I know you have never worked for Ketcham, boy. Now, be careful not to commit yourself. What was this money given to you for doing?"

Darry smiled as he drew out a paper.

How fortunate that the hardware merchant who sold traps and purchased such furs as were taken in that region had insisted upon giving him a little bill of sale, in order to bind the transaction, and prove conclusively what the reigning price happened to be at the time.

"Please glance at that, sir."

Darius Quarles did so, and a shade of disappointment crossed his face.

"I see you have taken up the same foolish pursuit that young Joe Peake followed—wasting your time loafing in the marsh when you had better be going to school and perhaps learning to become a useful man, a lawyer like myself for instance."

Darry shrugged his shoulders, and his action brought a frown to the face of the narrow-minded man who sat there before him; perhaps he jumped to the conclusion that this frank-faced lad did not entertain such an exalted notion of his greatness as he would have liked to impress upon him.

"At least that proves I did not steal the money, Mr. Quarles?" asked Darry.

"I suppose so, though it is an open question as to whether you have any right to take these little inoffensive animals, and sell their coats to Ketcham. I think he might be in a better business; but then he always was a cruel boy."

As Darry remembered the hardware man he believed him to be a jolly, red-faced man, and with a kindly eye, quite the opposite from the fishy orb of Mr. Quarles; but then there are some things that had better remain unsaid, and he did not try to voice his opinion.

"Then you will not do Mrs. Peake this little favor, sir?" he asked.

"Business is business with me, young man. Sometimes it is one person's day, and then the tables turn, and it is another's. This happens to be my time. According to the strict construction of the law, and the wording of the mortgage, the failure to pay the interest on time, with three days' grace, constitutes a lien on the property. I have a use for that cottage—in fact, a relative of mine fancies it. Here, I will give Nancy a chance to redeem her home. Wait a minute or two."

He wrote rapidly on a sheet of paper, signed the same, and held it out.

"Seven days I agree to wait, and if the principal and delayed interest are not handed over to me by next Tuesday, just one week from to-day, on Wednesday they will have to vacate. That will do, boy. Tell Nancy I only do that because of our old friendship. Had it been anyone else they would have cleared out before this. You can go now."

Darry had to bite his lips harder than ever to keep from telling the skinflint just what he thought of him.

Thrusting the paper in his pocket he stalked from the den of the human spider, his mind in a whirl; but grimly determined to try and find some means for saving the humble home of Abner Peake from the hand of the spoiler.

CHAPTER XVII: ABNER TELLS A LITTLE HISTORY

As he walked home that evening Darry was figuring. Fourteen dollars was not going far when the sum required, according to the figures Mr. Quarles had written out, reached the grand total of a hundred and eleven dollars and thirty-seven cents.

He had had much more than that on board the poor old Falcon when she went to pieces, the amount of his savings for several years; but there was no use of his thinking about that.

To whom could he look for assistance?

He had not a friend, save new ones in the village; and even Mr. Keeler would be apt to decline to lend him money. Times were hard, collections very slow—he had heard this said many times of late—and to small merchants the sum of a hundred dollars means much.

Darry thought it best not to say anything just then to Mrs. Peake, though a little later he must tell her about his visit to the money lender, and deliver the message Mr. Quarles had sent to her.

He was due to cross the sound on the morrow, and perhaps it would be best to tell Abner first; he might have been making some arrangement to get someone else to assume the mortgage, and pay the lawyer off.

So Darry tried to assume a cheerfulness he was far from feeling.

Long he lay awake that night, thinking and trying to lay out some plan of action that might promise results.

In the morning Darry visited his traps.

Only one victim rewarded his labor, and this added to his gloom.

He finished all his various chores, and they were many, for he had taken numerous duties upon his shoulders in order to spare Abner's wife.

As before, it was nearly the middle of the afternoon before he could get away.

Mr. Keeler loaded him down with packages intended for the station-keeper; indeed Darry had to make two trips between the store and his boat before he had all his cargo aboard.

The weather was what a sailor would call "dirty"; that is, it gave promise of turning into more or less of a storm, and wise mariners would be keeping a weather eye out for a safe and snug harbor.

Darry had no fear. He believed he knew that bay like a book now, and since he had tinkered with the boat and placed it in fair condition he thought it could stand any sea that might meet him in his passage to and fro between the mainland and the stretch of sand acting as a buffer to the ocean tides.

It was a dead calm when he started, and he was compelled to use the oars; but by the time he reached the middle a breeze sprang up, and quick to take advantage of his opportunity he spread his bit of a sail, and went flying along like a frightened gull.

Abner was always glad to see him, and taking advantage of the first chance to get the life saver alone, Darry told of his recent experience with the loan shark.

The other looked very downcast; indeed, Darry could not remember having ever seen him appear so disheartened.

"It means trouble for the poor ole woman, Darry. If I kin only muster up enough courage to ask some o' the folks to help me out p'raps we kin pull through; but the best o' friends pull back wen money is spoken of. They all got ther own burdens to kerry. I know I war a fool to ever do it; but Jenny got on my nerves yuh see, an' promised to give it back. An' thet shark, Quarles, it does him a lot o' good to know he kin push me down a peg," he said, with a heavy sigh.

"I seemed to get the notion that he didn't love you very much, Mr. Peake," remarked Darry.

"I thort he'd forgot all about it, but now I know he ain't, the skunk! He holds it agin me, and hes all these years. I reckon he jest hugged hisself wen I kim to him an' asked that loan. It war jest like playin' into his hands. Yuh see, lad, him an' me was rivals onct on a time."

Darry pricked up his ears.

Here was a touch of romance, something one would hardly expect to find in connection with so ordinary looking a man as Abner Peake.

"You mean that he wanted Nancy—that is Mrs. Peake, to marry him?" he asked.

"Thet's jest it, son. I reckon he'd a got her, too, fur I didn't hold a candle to Darius wen it kim to looks or larnin', but yuh see thet's whar chanct stepped in an' guv me a shove."

"Something happened then?"

"Nancy fell overboard off a boat we was all on. Darius, he didn't know how to swim and all he could do was to yell and wave his arms."

"And you went overboard after her?"

"I reckon I did. They sed as how I was in the water nigh about as quick as Nancy herself. She was a carryin' on high, like she was chokin', when I got to her, but I had her out in a jiffy. Arter thet she kinder took to me, an' Darius he got the mitten."

"Now I understand why he feels that way toward you," said Darry, wisely.

"They was some things I never did understand 'bout that thing. Nancy, she was allers the best gal swimmer in the village, but she did act like she was drownin' that day. Some sed as how they thort she tumbled over apurpose jest to hev some fun, an' see which o' her beaux'd drap in arter her the quickest," and the surfman smiled at the thought.

"And you won out. I guess Mr. Quarles has never forgiven you for that. But what can be done to beat him at his game now? Isn't there any way?"

"We got a week to try, an' as I git off before the end o' the time I'll see if anything kin be did. P'rhaps Keeler might help me out, though I did hear him say he was mighty hard up jest now. It was nice in yuh tryin' to do wot yuh did, boy. I knowed I wasn't makin' no mistake when I sized yuh up as the right sorter lad to take leetle Joey's place."

The life saver put an arm affectionately across the shoulders of his companion, and Darry never felt prouder in his life than when he realized that he had "made good" with this simple surfman who had been so kind to him at their first meeting.

"I only wish I had been able to do what I wanted to. It it had been any other man but Mr. Quarles I think he would have fixed it up, and I meant to put aside what I earned this winter, either from trapping or working for Mr. Singleton, to wipe out all that debt. I will yet, if I have the chance, and you can get somebody to take over the mortgage," he said, stoutly.

"Give me time to think, lad. Wen yuh kim acrost another time p'raps I'll have some plan made up. I'd do nigh anything to save pore Nancy bein' put outen our leetle home. 'Taint much to look at, but she sets a heap by it, I reckon. And as soon as I git a chanct I mean to drop outen this business an' try to make a livin' another way, so I kin be home more. Fishin' it might be, er somethin' thet way."

That night Darry played for the men, but they could not help noticing that much of his music was along the sad order.

In the morning the sky was still overcast, and the sound lay in a bank of half darkness that looked like fog, though the whistling wind seemed to forbid such a thing.

Abner was a little dubious about letting the boy depart, but Darry laughed at the idea of any harm befalling him.

He had several things he wished to attend to, and besides, Mrs. Peake would need him through the day in many ways.

He entered his boat and took up the oars for a hard row, for the wind was of too deceptive a character to allow him to make use of his sail.

The men of the station had come down to see him off, for by this time Darry had won his way into the hearts of every rough fellow, and they looked upon him as a sort of general ward of the crew, pulled out of the sea at their door and destined for great things.

Not one of them but who believed a bright future awaited Peake's new boy, and many were the predictions made among them, some even venturing the assertion that he would be president yet.

So they waved their sou'westers and shouted a merry good-bye to him as he rowed into the gray blanket of mist that shrouded the sound.

CHAPTER XVIII: THE IMPRISONED LAUNCH

The prospect ahead did not dismay Darry at all.

He had been a sailor for some years and was accustomed to meeting all kinds of bad weather.

Besides, his boat though old, was staunch, and could hold its own against waves that would upset another craft less steady; and then again he knew how to handle his oars with the skill that only long practice can bring.

By degrees he lost sight of the sandy shore.

He was now surrounded by a heaving sheet of water, and it required all his knowledge of things nautical to keep his bearings, for it was impossible to see even the slightest object on any side.

The situation would have alarmed many a lad less accustomed to depending on himself in emergencies.

Darry felt no fear.

He noted the direction of the waves, and unless the wind shifted suddenly, which it was not apt to do, he felt positive he could bring up somewhere along the shore near the village.

To his surprise he heard the sullen boom of a gun close by and wondered what any sportsman could be doing out there in that dense atmosphere, where it was impossible to see more than fifty feet away.

Certainly ducks could not be coming to stool under such conditions.

What could he be firing at then?

There it was again, one shot following another in rapid order, until he had counted six.

That would indicate the possession of one of those new style repeating shotguns, capable of holding half a dozen shells, and worked with a pump action.

All of a sudden it struck Darry that possibly someone was in trouble and was taking this means of summoning assistance; though the chances were very slight that any bayman would be anywhere near with that gray blanket covering things—they knew enough to stick to the shore at such a time.

Our hero changed his course a little thinking it could do no harm to look into matters and see what the bombarding meant.

Should it prove that some green sportsman from one of the clubs was lost in the mist perhaps he would be glad of help, and might even promise to pay liberally to be taken ashore in tow.

Just then Darry's mind was filled with an eager desire to make money, for he knew of a good use to which he could put it.

Again as he approached, the rattle of a fusilade came to his ears, followed by a series of shouts in a strained voice.

He was close on the spot apparently.

"Hello!" he shouted in return.

An answering whoop came back.

"This way, please! I'm in a peck of trouble here!" he heard someone say.

Twisting his head around as he bobbed up and down on the rollers, our hero caught just a glimpse of some object that seemed stationary, with the waves breaking over it.

It was even worse than being lost upon the sound then—the unknown had driven his boat upon some half hidden rocks, and caught as in a vise she was in danger of being wrecked unless some other craft came upon the spot and pulled her off.

That accounted for the shots and shouts, her owner realizing his extreme peril, for he was two miles from land and the storm increasing constantly.

Darry pushed on and soon another surprise awaited him.

"Hello! is that you, Darry?" asked a voice, and now he recognized it, so that even before he turned around again he knew he was once more in the company of Paul Singleton.

"How are you, sir?" he cried. "Looks like you had run aground in the middle of the bay. If you will give me a rope I'll try and drag you off the way you went on. That is the only thing to be done."

"I like the way you go about business," answered the young man. "I begin to have hopes that my poor little Griffin may come out of this adventure with a whole skin. It began to look as though I might have to swim for it. Here you are with the painter, which I have fastened to the stern. All depends on how good a haul you can give, Darry."

"What happened to your engine, sir?" asked the boy, surprised that it was not working in the effort to help the boat off.

"I'll start it up again, but it did no good before, only churned the water. It seems I am wedged between two rocks so fast that even the lift of the waves has no effect upon the boat. They break all over us, and I'm wet to the skin and shivering in the bargain. You're as welcome as the flowers in May, Darry."

The engine was speedily started up and the little propeller thrashed the water at a great rate, but though the cedar craft trembled violently there was no change in her position.

"Keep that up and stay in the stern, so as to lighten the bow all you can. I think that is where she is caught fast. If you have anything heavy up forward and can manage to shift it aft so much the better," called Darry, as he kept off by an expert use of the oars; indeed, Paul never could understand how he managed to do this and secure the rope to a thwart at the same time.

"There are a few things up there I can move—the water can and a lot of stuff in tins. Will you be able to hold out a few minutes longer?" asked Paul.

"Easy enough. Take your own time, sir. When you're ready tell me, and I'll give a series of sharp jerks. I hope we can make her move some."

Presently the owner of the motor-boat declared he had moved everything possible, and that the bow seemed to be a little more free than before, as though almost ready to rise with each flowing wave that swept past with a rush.

Darry set to work and began to use every atom of strength in his sturdy muscles; at the same time he engineered matters in such a clever fashion that every time he pulled his oars through the water it was with a rapid movement in the nature of a shock, so that the little hawser tightening, gave a drag at the imprisoned craft.

"She's moving!" yelled Paul Singleton, excitedly.

Darry kept right along, pulling with even more vim than before.

"Bully boy! she's coming! I can feel her move each time. If only an inch, it is something. We're going to get her off! It's a cinch, I tell you!"

Plainly Paul Singleton was considerably excited over the changed prospect that confronted him, and his cries gave the lad heart to exert himself to the utmost.

Suddenly he found that he was towing the launch behind him.

She had left her berth in between the two rocks and floated on the waves.

The owner gave a last whoop of delight.

"I knew if anyone could accomplish it, you would. I think you must be my good genius, Darry. To think of our meeting again here in the middle of the bay and just when I was on my way to your home to see if I could induce you to keep your half-given promise. It's great! Tell me about destiny after this."

That was the way Paul was calling out, as he busied himself in righting things aboard the jaunty little cedar craft.

SHE HAD left HER BERTH IN BETWEEN THE TWO ROCKS AND FLOATED ON THE WAVES.

"Now, what's to hinder you coming aboard and towing the rowboat astern? The engine is all right and capable of twelve miles an hour, so we can go with this blow easily enough," he suggested.

Darry was quite willing, for his arms felt a bit weary after his exerions, and the launch did look comfortable, even though fairly drenched just then, as a result of the waves breaking over the stern while she was held a prisoner in the jaws of rock.

The transfer was made without any particular trouble, and once Darry had secured his boat to the brass cleat in the stern of the launch he set to work throwing some of the surplus water overboard.

"Working your passage, eh?" laughed Paul, who seemed to be in unusually high spirits, such was the re-action that had come over him.

Meanwhile they drew in toward the land.

What with the rain that was falling both of them were wet through; but this was such a chronic condition for a sailor lad to be in that Darry, for one, paid little attention to it.

CHAPTER XIX: THE PART OF AN ELDER BROTHER

"Come," said Paul, after the boat had been tied up where the waves could not reach them and things had begun to assume a more comfortable aspect; "Here's a fine little cabin and an oil stove on which to make a hot pot of coffee, besides assisting to dry us out. I insist on you staying to keep me company for a while. We are both cold and wet. Say you will, Darry!"

Darry did not need much urging. He was wet and chilled, and it did look cozy after Paul had started the stove going.

"Besides," continued Paul, misconstruing his silence; "I am under heavy obligations to you for coming to my assistance when you did. You saved my life and you are a regular life saver like Mr. Peake. There must be some way in which I can partly cancel that debt. You are allowed salvage by law when you save a vessel, Darry, did you know it? But for your coming my poor little Griffin must have gone to pieces, not to mention what would have become of her owner. Now, how can I settle for this indebtedness."

He was laughing as he spoke, but Darry considered the moment had come for him to put in a plea for his friends.

So he swallowed what seemed to be a lump in his throat, for after all it was no easy thing to ask such a favor from one who was hardly more than a stranger.

"Mr. Singleton, I was just wishing I could meet you somewhere soon," he began.

"Well, that is queer, since I was thinking about you too, and hoping you would not go back on me, for somehow, I seem to have set my mind on having you with me. And besides, there was another reason why I wanted to keep track of you, which I may tell you some day soon, Darry. But why were you wanting to see me?"

"To ask a great favor?"

"Not to let you off from your promise?"

"Oh, no, I'll be only too glad of a chance to be with you. It would be glorious to spend some time aboard this fine little boat. What I wanted to say—that is, the favor I wanted to ask was not for myself."

"Come, that's rather strange, Darry. Not for yourself—a favor for another? Let's hear what it's about. You've certainly excited my curiosity, and don't hesitate a bit about it. I shall be only too willing to do anything that lies in my power, if it pleases you."

The words were most kind, and the smile that accompanied them even more so.

Darry flushed with a sense of coming victory, for something told him he was in line to win out, and that the money-shark would be cheated of his prey.

"I want to borrow a hundred dollars, sir," he said, slowly.

Paul laughed as if amused.

Immediately taking out his pocket-book he withdrew from it a bank bill of a large denomination and handed it to his companion, who received it in an embarrassed way.

"There you are, Darry, and there is no loan about it. I owe you many times that much for your assistance. Now, don't say anything about it, for I am not used to being crossed. It's a mere bagatelle to me, as you must know. Some time if you feel like it you may tell me the circumstances that have arisen; but not until you're good and ready. I'm only too delighted to be of a little help."

"I'm going to tell you all about it right here. It's only fair you should know where your money is going, sir. As soon as I get my breath you shall hear," went on Darry, fingering the hundred dollar bill as though he could hardly believe his senses.

Never did a bill of like denomination seem to carry more happiness in its touch; he could easily picture the light that would dawn upon the worried features of Mrs. Peake when he handed her that mortgage, canceled, and Abner, too, how he would be likely to throw up his hat in the air and shout like a boy.

Paul Singleton had been observing him curiously, but with kindling eyes, as if he saw more and more in this boy to admire; he could give something of a guess as to what was coming, and hence was not much surprised a little later when he heard the story of Darius Quarles and his long-slumbering revenge.

He laughed heartily at the quaint way in which Abner had hinted about Nancy tumbling overboard on purpose, in order to discover which of her lovers was the better man.

"I've met the lady, and to tell the truth I really believe she would have been equal to such a prank some years back. There's a lurking spirit of mischief in her eyes to this day, though I know she has met with a great grief lately, for I heard all about poor little Joe," Paul said, after Darry had finished.

"You can never understand how glad I am to be able to bring a little joy to this poor couple. They have not known much happiness, sir. Even now, Abner is compelled to be away from home all the time in order to earn bread for his family."

Paul Singleton seemed to consider.

"We'll talk that over later on, Darry, when we have plenty of time," he answered. "Perhaps I may be able to suggest a remedy. I have shares in several properties down this way, and possibly Abner can be given a steady job as keeper at the club, or put in charge of a farm I own not far away from here. Depend upon it, some means can be found to help your benefactor out. I'd rather talk about you, just now, and what you have seen in your adventurous past. In fact, I'd like to know everything that ever happened to you, if you don't mind," he continued.

Again Darry had that queer sensation pass over him, and he could not but remember what Abner had said about the possibility of his finding out something connected with his childhood, and that this young gentleman would be the means of supplying the missing link.

So as they sat there and sipped the delicious coffee and dried out in comfort, he answered all the questions Paul could think of asking.

They covered his entire past, from his earliest recollection, and especially about the old man who had finally deserted him in Naples, for he naturally occupied a prominent place in the recital.

Darry had called him uncle, but thought the man could not have held that relationship toward him. He never knew what had become of the old man, but suspected that he must have met with some fatal accident in the Italian city.

Then he narrated how he had supported himself by playing the violin, and at the same time learned to speak Italian as well as a native.

Finally came the scene in the café, when Captain Harley rescued him from the cruelty of a bully, and after that there was very little to tell up to the time the brigantine was lost and his best friend vanished from the scene, never to appear again on earth.

Paul Singleton harked back to his earliest recollections, and with the skill of a lawyer asked questions that put Darry's memory to a strain; he examined the singular mark upon the boy's arm with deepest interest and seemed impressed.

"That will undoubtedly prove one thing or the other, as soon as I can see her," Darry heard him say, as if to himself.

Evidently Paul Singleton knew nothing of the mark and was depending upon some other party to settle the identification.

It was noon before either of them realized it.

Darry declared he must hurry off so as to catch the lawyer at his office and settle matters before going home.

"Hark, Darry," said Paul, holding his hand as they parted; "promise me that if there is anything else I can do to please you I'm to know it right away. Confide in me, my boy. It makes me happy to share, even to a limited extent, in your little affairs. And you know we are going to be great chums all winter, you and I. Look on me then as a sort of elder brother or a cousin, if you please."

And Darry thought as he looked into the clear laughing eyes of Paul Singleton that nothing would give him greater happiness on earth than if he could claim relationship to this fine manly fellow.

He seemed to be walking on air as he left the cove and headed into the village.

Upon calling at the office of Darius Quarles he was disappointed to learn that the lawyer had gone off in his closed buggy early that morning, and would not be back all day—he had to foreclose a mortgage the clerk remarked, and never allowed that duty to be performed by a subordinate, for it gave him too much satisfaction to attend to it personally.

Even his employees had a secret contempt for his mean ways, it seemed.

"He expects to be home to supper, and if your business is pressing you might call at his house, which is just out of the village on the road to Harden," the young clerk said in concluding.

"Thank you, I believe I shall call, as I wish to see him very much," replied Darry, and left the place.

He made his way along the rather lonely road that led to the humble home of the Peakes, bowing his head to the storm, and yet with a song of thanksgiving swelling in his heart, for he knew he was carrying with him the means of lifting the load that had for some time oppressed his kind benefactors.

Suddenly something struck him a stunning blow and looking up as he staggered he heard a chorus of shrill laughs, and realized that a rope had been thrown around him in such a way that his arms were pinioned down at his sides.

At the same moment several impish figures sprang out of the dense brush and fell upon him with vicious blows, as though bent upon knocking him down.

Though they had their faces concealed after a ridiculous fashion he recognized the malicious laugh of one as belonging to Jim Dilks.

CHAPTER XX: BAD LUCK AND GOOD

Of course Darry knew what this attack meant.

His enemy had been brooding over matters for a long time, and despairing of accomplishing his end while Darry was armed with a gun, during his daily visits to the big marsh, he had finally decided to lie in wait and have it out on the road from the village.

Jim wisely backed himself up with a couple of allies in thus undertaking to give his enemy that long-delayed whipping.

He had tried it once by himself and apparently had no relish to repeat the experiment.

Perhaps it would have been the part of wisdom on the part of the young life saver to have taken to his heels and beat a masterly retreat.

Great generals have done this same thing and considered it no dishonor to save their army for another day.

To a high-spirited lad, however, it is the last thought, and many a fellow will stand the chances of a beating rather than to turn his back on the foe.

Of course there was no time to consider the matter.

The three disguised boys attacked him on all sides, and almost before Darry knew what he was doing blows were being exchanged with a vim.

He fought gallantly and well, sending in just as many hard hits as his knowledge of the game permitted.

Whenever he saw an opening he was quick to take advantage of the same, and as a consequence first one of Jim's supporters and then the other temporarily bit the dust, with a galaxy of stars floating before their mental vision.

They were very much surprised.

True, they may have heard something about the fighting abilities of this wonderful new boy; but Jim had kept declaring that only for his lame hand he would surely have easily come out victor on that memorable day of the first meeting, and they were forced to believe him.

Artful Jim was wise enough to do a great deal of jumping about, but seemed quite willing his allies should meet with the brunt of the battle while he saved himself for the finishing touches.

When Darry had tired himself out against Sim Clark and Bowser then his time would have arrived.

Darry anticipated being whipped in the encounter.

It was not to be expected that one boy could hold his own against three such tough customers as those opposed to him, since they would wear him out.

Nevertheless, he declined to run at the beginning, and after a little it was entirely out of the question for him to do so, since he lacked the wind to conduct a flight.

So there was really nothing to do but stand and take what was coming to him, at the same time give as good as he knew how.

They would never be able at any rate to say they had won an easy victory.

By this time they were beautifully daubed with mud, as each appeared to be the under dog while the minutes crept along.

Darry's only hope lay in the possibility of some one passing that way, and as the day was so stormy, and few people ever took this road, his chances were indeed slender.

Now the whole bunch seemed to be upon the ground alongside the road, struggling like a pack of Kilkenny cats, the three aggressors having their hands on Darry at one time in the endeavor to subdue him.

Suddenly Jim gave a hoarse cry.

"Haul off dere, fellers; somebody's comin'!" was what he ejaculated.

Immediately the other two sprang to their feet like a couple of deer, afraid lest they be caught at their game; perhaps a vision of old Hank Squires flashed before them, with the penitentiary in the background.

Darry, out of breath, but game to the last, made an ineffectual attempt to hold one of his tormentors, catching the flying end of his jacket; but such was the moment of Sim's upward movement, and the flimsy character of his wearing apparel, that the entire section came away, remaining in the grip of the enemy as he went tearing after his mates.

The three of them plunged into the bushes alongside the road, and were lost to sight, leaving Darry half sitting up on the road, plastered with mud, and ruefully surveying the strip of cloth in his hand.

After all it proved to be a false alarm, for no one came in sight.

Darry was not foolish enough to invite a further attack by remaining on the ground after the enemy had temporarily withdrawn, so he gathered himself together and continued along the road, feeling of his limbs to ascertain just how seriously he had been bruised, and trying to scrape some of the mud from his clothes.

He felt ashamed to let Mrs. Peake see him in this condition, for the clothes had been Joe's, and naturally she would feel badly to discover how they were now treated to a coating of mud.

But then the fact of his having such a joyful surprise for her would discount any bad effect of his appearance.

Thinking thus, Darry put his hand eagerly into the inside pocket where he had so carefully stowed the little leather pocket-book in which the hundred dollar bill given him by Paul, as well as the amount which his muskrat pelts had fetched at the hardware store, had been lodged.

The pocket-book was gone!

Poor Darry shivered as if someone had struck him a blow.

Could he have lost it while upon the shore with Paul Singleton and had the angry sound claimed it as passage money for having allowed a victim to escape?

No, he recollected very distinctly feeling it there as he started from the office of the lawyer, after learning that Mr. Quarles was away.

Then it must have fallen out during his struggles on the road, for several times he had been on his back, with those "wildcats" clawing at him.

Despite the chances of meeting them again, and having the struggle renewed, he deliberately turned back and quickly ran to the spot where there were plain evidences to be seen of the free-for-all fight.

How eagerly he searched every foot of that territory, his heart, figuratively speaking, in his throat with anxiety. But as the minutes passed and he realized the hopeless character of his hunt it seemed to drop like lead into his shoes, the change was so great.

Then there remained only one solution of the mystery—one of those young rascals must have inserted a hand in his coat while they were struggling there on the road and stolen the pocket-book with its contents.

His heart seemed almost broken, and he even contemplated rushing after them to renew the battle and tear the prize from their possession; but a little thought caused him to understand how foolish such a move would be, for he had no idea as to what quarter they could he heading for when they left him, unless it might be that shack in the swamp, and it would be rash indeed for him to go there alone.

He tried to pluck up courage enough to go home, basing all his hopes on Paul, who had seemed so very kind, and ready to help him out.

Of course Mrs. Peake was astonished at his appearance, but the rising anger vanished when she learned who had been the cause of his misfortunes—at least it was turned in the direction of Jim Dilks, and she vowed that before another day had passed she would swear out a warrant for his arrest, and go personally to see that Hank Squires did his duty.

Depressed in spirits Darry crept away to change his clothes for some others she brought him, also once belonging to Joe.

Mrs. Peake advised that the muddy garments be hung up until they dried, when by a vigorous brushing they might be restored to something like their former condition of cleanliness.

Accordingly, Darry first of all picked up the trousers and placed them on a line in a corner of the room, where they could drip without soiling the floor, he having spread a newspaper beneath.

Then he proceeded to attend to the coat in the same way.

While engaged in this he felt something bulky in one of the pockets and smiled faintly as he remembered thrusting that portion of Sim's torn coat there.

This he had done under the impression that Hank might consider it conclusive evidence, calculated to convict the young ruffian beyond a possibility of doubt.

It might just as well hang alongside the other garments, though Darry did not intend removing the incriminating mud stains from the fragment.

As he drew the offending piece of cloth out he was thrilled to feel something in the folds, and with trembling fingers he opened it out.

It seemed that with the portion of the coat that had come away in his hands was one of the pockets, and out of this receptacle Darry quickly drew something at which he stared as though he fancied he were dreaming.

His pocket-book!

Sim had undoubtedly snatched the same from his person as they wrestled upon the ground, and having no other place in which to hide it at the moment, had thrust it in the very outside pocket of his coat that a minute later remained in the grip of the boy he had robbed.

Darry stared at it until he realized the amazing fortune that had so kindly returned him his property, and then rolling over on the floor he shook with wild laughter, so that Mrs. Peake came to the door in alarm to see if he were ill.

CHAPTER XXI: SATISFYING THE MORTGAGE

While Darry was gurgling with laughter, still clutching the fragment of coat and the precious pocket-book, he felt a hand seize his arm.

Looking up he saw the puzzled and anxious face of Abner's wife.

"What ails you, boy? Did they injure you more than you told me?" she asked, as if fearful that he were going out of his mind.

To the further astonishment of the good woman the boy climbed to his feet, suddenly threw his arms around her neck and gave her a vigorous hug.

"It's all right, mother, after all; they didn't get it!" he exclaimed.

"What's all right? I don't understand at all," she replied, looking at the dirty strip of cloth he was holding, and the pocket-book as well.

"Why, what do you think, while we were struggling there on the road, with me underneath part of the time, that sneak thief, Sim Clark, managed to steal my pocket-book out of my inner pocket. That was what made me seem so blue, for I had something in it I meant to show you. But when he tried to run away I held on and part of his coat ripped away. I stuck it in my pocket, thinking Hank would like to see it as evidence, and when I took it out here, don't you see I found what I had lost in Sim's pocket! Did you ever hear of such luck in your born days."

Mrs. Peake herself laughed.

"You do seem to be a fortunate boy. And they would have robbed you of what little you have. I'm glad you got it back, and I'm determined to see Hank Squires to-morrow about this thing. It has gone far enough."

"But I've got something else to tell you. Come and sit down where we can talk," he continued, feeling happier than ever before in all his life, for he knew he was in a condition to chase away the clouds that had been bringing anxiety to her mind for months.

So he told first of all about his visit to the hardware man, and how he obtained fourteen dollars for his muskrat skins.

After that came the call upon the lawyer and what followed in connection with his offer to pay the interest due, and how Mr. Quarles had absolutely refused to accommodate him.

Nancy sighed as she heard what the cold, grasping man of law had said about settling old scores.

Perhaps she was sorry now she had given him such cause for hatred; but better the life she had led than one as the wife of a cruel money shark of his breed.

From this Darry soon branched out and spoke of his trip to the shore, and how on his return a kindly fate had allowed him to be of material assistance to the very young man with whom he expected to spend the winter on his launch.

Mrs. Peake began to listen more eagerly now, for she surmised that something of a pleasant nature was coming.

When Darry finally placed the money in her hand, she looked at it in bewilderment, never having touched so much at one time in all her life; then she turned her tear-stained eyes upon him, and drawing him into her motherly arms kissed him again and again.

And Darry never felt so well repaid for any action of his life as that.

There was sunshine in the Peake house the balance of that day, even though the weather without was dark and overcast, for light hearts carry an atmosphere of their own that does not depend upon outside influences.

The woman would not hear of Darry's going to see the lawyer that night.

Something might happen to him again, with those malicious boys still at large, and it would be wiser she thought, to wait until morning, when the two of them could take the money to Darius Quarles and satisfy the mortgage.

Besides, Nancy thought she would like to see what the money-lender looked like when finding his plans frustrated so neatly.

"Thank goodness that relative of his will have to wait some time before this house falls into his clutches," she remarked, for the fourth time, since it was impossible, just then, to talk about anything else.

So when another day dawned, while the weather was still heavy they walked to the village and astonished the lawyer by appearing in his office soon after his arrival.

Supposing that Nancy had come to beg for more time, he set his face in its hardest lines, even though pretending to be sympathetic—times were out of joint, collections difficult to make, and he absolutely needed every cent he could scrape together in order to meet his obligations—that was the way he put it, when she announced she had come in relation to the mortgage.

"Then I suppose you will be glad to receive this money, Darius, and return the mortgage canceled to me. And you can be sure that Abner will never trouble you in the same way again," she said, thrusting the full sum, with interest toward him.

He slowly counted it, and found that every cent, as he had written it down for Darry, was there.

"Ahem! this is an unexpected pleasure, Nancy. I congratulate you, indeed I do, on your success in finding someone to take over the mortgage," he stammered, as his face turned from red to white, and his little eyes glittered.

"You are mistaken. There will be no mortgage on my home after this. The money has been earned by this brave boy here, not borrowed," she said, coldly.

This caused him to look at Darry, and his mouth told that he was gritting his teeth wrathfully.

"Ah! yes, indeed, truly a remarkable boy. What has he been doing now—taking the rats of the swamp by wholesale, I presume? Let me see, only yesterday he had sold twenty-six skins for fourteen dollars, and now a hundred dollar bill follows. It is amazing. Pardon me if I doubt my eyes. I suppose the bill is a good one?"

"We will wait here until you go and find out. You might ask Mr. Paul Singleton, who has a little launch down at the docks, and is a member of the club above," replied Mrs. Peake, with stinging emphasis.

"Did Mr. Singleton give him this money?" demanded the lawyer, suddenly.

"He did, for saving his launch out in the bay yesterday. And what is more, Darry expects to cruise with him the balance of the winter. He has taken a great fancy for my boy. You can find him easily if you wish to ask him about this."

It was wonderful how quickly the lawyer changed his manner.

He knew who Paul Singleton was, and what wealth he represented in the exclusive sporting club near Ashley.

"That alters the complexion of the whole thing. Now I congratulate Darry on his good fortune in making such a good, easy friend. Of course the bill must be all right if Paul Singleton gave it to him. I will immediately attend to the mortgage for you, and also see that it is satisfied on the books at the county office. Meanwhile I shall write you out a receipt in full, showing that it has been paid."

Mrs. Peake said nothing more.

She felt the utmost contempt for this man, and having been enabled to defeat his scheme for humiliating herself and husband, wished to remain in his company no longer than was absolutely necessary.

So she and Darry presently went forth, and how pure even the stormy atmosphere seemed after being for half an hour in that spider's web of a lawyer's den.

On the strength of the improved prospects Mrs. Peake felt that she was privileged to spend a portion of the small sum of money she had been hoarding against paying the interest, though as it had not amounted to the full sum she had not dared approach Darius with an offer.

Mr. Keeler, being a good friend of the Peakes, and inclined to be hostile to the lawyer, she naturally confided her late troubles to his sympathetic ear, feeling that she could not keep silent.

He shook the hand of the boy with sincerity, and declared that it was a great day for Abner and his brood when the surf man helped to pull the cabin boy of the Falcon out of the sea.

Being a modest lad, Darry escaped as soon as he could, and waited around until Mrs. Peake was ready to go home, when he showed up to carry her parcels.

The family feasted that night most royally.

Darry himself had purchased a steak in the store as his donation, and this was a luxury the little Peakes seldom knew.

Ducks and fish were all very well, together with oysters, when they could get them; but after all there was a sameness in the diet that rather palled on the appetite, and that beefsteak with onions did smell mighty fine, as even the good cook admitted.

The future looked very rosy to both Darry and Abner's wife.

When the latter heard what Paul Singleton had said about getting some place for the life saver ashore, where he could be with his family right along, the poor woman broke down and sobbed; but it was joy that caused the tears to flow, and Darry felt his own eyes grow wet as he realized how she must have suffered while compelled to live in this mean way.

Nancy having been a teacher had looked to better things, no doubt; but Abner thus far had lacked the ability to provide them for his family. Now, however, the current had changed.

"And to think it all comes through you, boy. God sent you to us, I believe, just when things were at the worst. How different it looks now. I am the happiest woman in Ashley this night," she declared, and it seemed as though she could hardly take her beaming eyes off his face during that whole evening as they sat and built air castles for the future.

It can be set down as certain that Darry found it hard to get to sleep after so much excitement. Long he lay there and went over all the recent experiences, to wonder again and again why Providence was so good to him, the waif who had until the last few years known only cuffs and trouble.

The morning showed no improvement in the weather, for which Darry was sorry, because he wished to cross the sound in order to carry the glorious news to Abner and relieve his mind of the worry that must even now fill it.

And as the prospect was that even worse weather might follow before it would improve he determined to go, though Mrs. Peake was rather loth to grant permission.

CHAPTER XXII: ABNER HEARS THE NEWS

When Darry reached the village and was making for the place where his boat was tied up, he remembered that Paul Singleton was close by with his motor-boat.

Perhaps he was aboard and would be interested in hearing what had happened to Darry since they parted.

Accordingly he walked that way and was accosted by a genial voice calling:

"All hail, comrade, what news? Come aboard. Just thinking about you, and if you hadn't hove in sight soon I meant to don my raincoat and saunter up to find out what was in the wind. Here you are, just in time to join me at my lunch, such as it is—coffee, a canoeist stew and some fresh bread I bought from a good housewife in the village. Sit down right there; no excuse, you must know sooner or later what sort of a cook I am, for we expect to share many a meal in common."

In such a hearty way did Paul Singleton greet him, and of course Darry had to obey orders, even though hardly hungry.

He entertained Paul with an account of his recent adventures, and that young gentleman nearly doubled up with merriment when he heard how a malicious fate had succeeded in cheating Sim Clark out of the reward of his villainy.

"And where are you off to now?" demanded Paul, when they had finished their "snack," as he termed it in Southern style, and Darry seemed to be getting ready to depart.

"Across to the station. Mr. Keeler told me last evening there was some important mail to go over, and I think its going to storm worse before it finally clears up."

"Looks pretty dusty out there even now, for your little tub. Say, suppose we take your boat in tow and go over in the launch? I was wondering what to do only a little while back. Besides, I've wanted to see the surfmen work their boat, and if it comes on to storm hard, perhaps there may be a necessity for them to launch. I'd be sorry to have a wreck occur; but if it does happen I'd like to be on hand. Say yes, now, Darry."

Of course he did, for who could resist Paul Singleton; especially when the passage could be made so much more quickly in the staunch little motor-boat than with his own clumsy craft.

In a short time they sallied out.

The cedar craft was a model of the boat builder's art, and carried a twelve-horse power engine, so that even though the wind and tide chanced to be against them they made steady progress toward the shore seen so dimly far across the sound.

Nearly every wave sent the spray flying high in the air as it struck the bow; but there was a hood to catch this, and besides both occupants of the motor-boat had donned oilskins before starting.

It was a long trip, nevertheless, for the wind continued to increase in force as the afternoon waned, and Darry, with a sailor's gift of foretelling what the weather was to be, predicted that the succeeding night must witness a storm such as had not visited the coast since the night he was cast ashore.

Abner was delighted to see his boy, and it was not long before the party found shelter in the warm station, for the air was growing bitter.

"A bad night ahead!" said one of the surfmen, after greeting Darry, "and worse luck, poor Tom here has broken his leg. Mr. Frazer is somethin' of a surgeon, and has set it, but as soon as this storm is over he must be taken home. It leaves us short a man if so be we are called out, unless some feller happens to run across before night, which is kinder unlikely."

"I'd be only too glad to pull an oar, if necessary, and you couldn't find any better man," said Darry, quickly, looking at Abner, who shook his head, dubiously.

"They may hev to take yuh, lad; but I hopes as how we aint gwine to be called out. It's a cruel night to fight the sea, an' only them as has been thar knows wot it means. Now come an' set down here, both on yuh, an' tell me all the news from hum. I seen somethin' in your eye, lad, thet tells me yuh knows sure a heap wuth hearin'. I hopes it's good news," he said.

"Indeed it is, the best ever," replied Darry, with bursting heart, and then as quickly as he could he told the whole story.

Poor Abner sat there, blinking, and hardly able to comprehend the wonderful change that had so suddenly come over his fortunes.

Unable to speak he could only stretch out his hand to Paul, and then turning to our hero looked at him with his very soul in his eyes.

After a little, when he became calmer, he asked many questions, and even had a quiet little laugh at the expense of Darius Quarles.

"That's the second time yuh see he's ben knocked out a-tryin' to rob me. Nancy done it fust a-fallin' into the water, and this time Darry here cum to the front. Darius he must be concludin' he was borned under an unlucky star, 'specially wen he tackles Nancy Peake. I'd give somethin' to see the gal jest now," he added wistfully as he tried to picture what she must look like when really and truly happy.

Long they talked, until an early supper was ready, and the men gathered about the table, while the wind shrieked and sighed about the corners of the station, telling of the severe labors the coming night would demand.

After the meal was finished nothing would do but that Darry must give them some music ere the first detail went out on their arduous duties in facing the cold storm.

Paul had known nothing of this accomplishment on the part of his new friend

He sat there as though enthralled while Darry drew such weird strains from the little polished instrument in his hands that this young man, who had doubtless listened to many masters of the violin believed he had never in all his life heard such wonderful music.

Of course the strange surroundings had something to do with it, for there was a constant accompaniment of howling wind, with the surge of the wild surf beating time to the magic of the bow, and it seemed as though the player selected just such music as would be appropriate to such a setting.

Finally the first detail had to make ready for their long tramp along the beach, and muffled in their oilskins they sallied forth.

Later on Abner and his companions expected to start out, for Paul was determined to learn all he could about this hard life of those who patrolled the coasts while the storms raged, a helpful auxiliary to the lighthouse department.

The men should have sought rest and sleep while they had the chance, but no one seemed desirous of lying down.

Tom, the poor fellow with the broken leg, was bearing up bravely, and only bemoaned the fact that, if there should be any necessity for the launching of the surfboat he could not do his duty.

Suddenly everyone started up.

Above the roar of the storm a sound had come that could not be anything other than the boom of a gun.

There is nothing that startles more than this sound, heard upon the shore as the storm rages, for it invariably tells of peril hovering over some vessel that has been beaten from her track and is threatened with wreck, either upon the reefs or the treacherous sands.

Instantly all was bustle and excitement.

Every man donned his oilskins, and as they had made all preparations there was little time wasted in doing this.

Paul rushed out with the rest, eager to be "in the swim," as he said.

It was a scene never to be forgotten.

The waves were running high and breaking upon the beach with a thunderous roar, while the wind added to the clamor; so that save for the absence of thunder and lightning the picture seemed to be a duplicate of that other so strongly impressed upon Darry's mind.

Down the beach they could catch glimpses of an illumination, and it seemed as though some of the coast patrol might be burning coster lights to signal the vessel on the reef.

Presently they would come back, when the lifeboat would be launched.

With material that was kept ready for just such an emergency a fire was immediately started.

Mr. Frazer was looking anxiously down the beach, and Darry heard him calling to Abner.

"I don't like the looks of things yonder. That fire is none of the work of our men. Jim Dilks and his wreckers must be over here looking for pickings. I pity any poor wretch who comes ashore and falls into their hands. That scoundrel wouldn't be above robbing a castaway, and even chocking out what little life remained in his body, if so be it looked like he might tell. Keep a lookout for the rascals, boys. And all give a hand here to get the boat out of the shed. We're going to have a hard night of it, I'm afraid."

CHAPTER XXIII: DARRY IN THE LIFEBOAT

The boat was soon rolled out and placed where it could be quickly launched at the word.

Mr. Frazer was not only the keeper of the station but the helmsman of the lifeboat, which latter was a most responsible position, since he must direct the movements of the men who pulled the oars, bring the boat under the vessel in peril, manage to rescue as many of those aboard as could be carried, and finally navigate the craft successfully to the shore.

Darry looked upon him as a wonderful man, a hero, indeed, whose equal he had never known.

There were signs of distress seaward. Through his night glasses Mr. Frazer reported seeing a steamer in trouble. She had evidently gone on the reef, having gotten out of her course in the wild storm, or else because the wreckers further down the coast had deceived her navigator by means of false beacons.

No matter, she was fast upon the treacherous reef and would likely fill and be a wreck before morning, since her entire port side seemed exposed to the fury of the waves.

It was a wonder how anything could remain on board and endure so terrific a pounding; if later on she were washed free the chances were there would be holes enough in her by that time to cause her to sink like a shot.

The lifeboat could not get out to her any too soon.

Those on board were burning lights, and sending up rocket after rocket to indicate that their need of assistance was great.

Still nothing could be done until the men on the detail came in.

Already it had been settled that unless assistance came speedily, in the shape of a recruit to take the place of Tom, Darry would have to go.

The boy was in a fever of suspense, fearful that he might be cheated out of the experience, as on the previous occasion.

Paul was quite useless because he knew so little about pulling an oar, while as a sailor, with some years experience on a vessel, Darry was at home on the water in any capacity.

"I certainly admire your grit, Darry," said Paul, shuddering as he looked out at the heaving waves, the white tops of which loomed up in the gloom.

"Oh! I'm used to these things. Dozens of storms I've been through, under all sorts of conditions," answered the boy.

"All the same it's a big risk. I hope nothing will go wrong. That's a mighty small boat to pit against the fury of the sea."

"But as safe as they make them. It's impossible to sink it, and the ropes are there to keep us from being swept out, even if flooded. All around the outside you see ropes, and if a fellow goes over he holds on to one of those until another wave sweeps him back in his seat again, and there you are."

Although Darry spoke so lightly it must not be assumed that he failed to realize the gravity attending the passage of the surboat out upon such a troubled sea; for accidents do happen to the crews of these life-saving craft, and many a daring soul has gone to his account while trying to rescue others.

But just then the patrol came running up, almost out of breath.

From one man Frazer learned that his surmise concerning the appearance of the lawless wreckers on the shore was well founded, and that they had been up to some mischief further south, where signs of lights had been noticed by this coastguard.

The word was given to take their places, as the boat was about to be launched.

They had waited a brief time to allow the newly-arrived men a chance to recover their wind for they would need it presently, when once upon the heaving bosom of the deep.

Paul squeezed the hand of his young friend.

How he envied him this chance to prove his courage and to pull an oar in a life-saving trip.

The rockets had ceased to ascend as though either the supply had given out, or else conditions had become so bad that there was no longer a chance to carry on this work.

Then came the word:

"Go!"

There was a simultaneous movement on the part of the entire crew, and as the sturdy men put their shoulders to the task the surfboat shot forward just at the proper instant when a wave expended itself upon the sloping beach.

Its prow entered the water, and those furthest ahead sprang into their places, whipping the long oars into the rowlocks for a struggle against the force of the next onrushing billow.

Darry was one of these.

He had not watched that other launching for nothing, and understood just what was required of him, as though through long practice.

Now they were off!

The oars dipped deep, and hardy muscles strained back of them.

Slowly but surely the boat gained against all the fury of the onrushing tide, and foot by foot they began to leave the shore.

Paul was shouting, swinging his hat, as Darry could see while he tugged at his task.

Once fully launched upon the swelling bosom of the sea, the progress of the surfboat was more rapid, though every yard had to be won by the most arduous of labor, the men straining like galley slaves under the lash; but in this case it was a sense of duty rather than the whip of the tyrant that urged them on.

No man but the helmsman saw anything of the steamer that was fast upon the cruel jaws of the reef, for it was against orders for anyone to turn his head.

Such an incautious movement might throw him out of balance in the swing of the stroke and bring about disaster, or at least temporarily disarrange their regular advance; they had to trust everything to the wisdom and experience of the man who hung on to the long steering oar, and blindly obey his shouted instructions.

Many times had he gone forth upon just such a hazard, and thus far his sagacity had proven equal to the task.

They began to hear human voices shrieking through the storm.

That meant they were drawing close under the lee of the steamer, and that those on board must have sighted them, and were consequently filled with new hope.

Above all else came the awful pounding of the sea upon the side of the doomed steamer.

Darry knew the sound well, for many a night had he gone calmly to sleep while the chorus of the elements was beating close to his head.

He had pulled well, and held his own with the brawny men of the crew, just as Mr. Frazer had known would be the case when he allowed him to take the place of Tom in the boat.

Abner was next to him, and the surfman had watched the manly efforts of his adopted boy with secret delight.

Few boys indeed of his size could have proven their worth to the crew of the lifeboat in time of need as Darry had done.

He could indeed be reckoned one of the life savers from this hour on, if so be they came back again to the shore that had witnessed their departure.

Now, as they swung around temporarily the rowers were afforded their first glimpse of the imperiled vessel.

It was undoubtedly a steamer, one of the coasters that pass up and down the Atlantic seaboard, bound from New York to one of the various southern ports, or vice versa, and usually keeping far enough out to avoid the perils that hover about Kitty Hawk and Hatteras.

She was in a bad position, having gone ashore, or been washed aground, so that her whole quarter was exposed to the sweep of the boiling sea.

Through the flying spray they could see numerous figures along the lee rail of the vessel, hanging on desperately, while now and then the water would sweep over the deck, and at such times a chorus of screams told that there were other than men there, women half frightened out of their senses by the peril.

The surfboat was, after some maneuvering, gotten in such a position under the lee of the steamer that a rope could be thrown aboard.

Then a woman was lowered by means of this, and safely stowed away.

As the rope had been fastened to the boat there was no longer necessity for the crew to strain at the oars, consequently they were at liberty to assist in caring for those sent down by the steamer's crew, working under the direction of a cool, level-headed captain.

Darry had cast off his oilskins, as being in the way.

A wetting was of small moment anyway to one so warm-blooded as he, and the cumbersome garments impeded his movements, since they were meant for a big man.

The sleeve of his shirt had also become torn in some way and flapped loose until he tucked it up out of the way.

All unconscious of the picturesque figure he made he continued to work with all his might, helping to receive the women and children as they were slipped over the side.

Many an eye was attracted toward him as seen by the light of the lanterns that were held over the side of the steamer to aid the workers, and more than one wondered how it came that a mere lad was to be found keeping company with these hardy men of the coast, seasoned to storms, and able to defy the rigors of the cold.

It was no easy task to take on a load of the passengers under such conditions.

Only when the surfboat rose on a billow could they be lowered, for at other times the distance was so great that the deck of the steamer looked as far away as the roof of a tall building.

Yet, thanks to the ability of the steamer captain, and the experience of the surfmen below, the shipping of the women and children was accomplished with but a single accident.

One child dropped off the rope, having been insecurely fastened, and with the shrieks of the women fell into the sea, but hardly had she reached the water than with a splash Darry was over, and had seized upon the little one.

His companions immediately reached out friendly hands, and both were drawn into the plunging boat, amid frantic cheers from all who had seen the daring rescue.

One woman seized hold of the boy as he pushed his way through the crowd to his place at the oars, and looked wildly in his face.

He supposed she must be the mother of the child he had saved, and not wishing for any scene just then, when he was needed at his place, as they were about to cast off, Darry gently broke her hold, leaving on her knees and staring after him.

Although he little suspected the fact it was something else that had chained the attention of this woman passenger; and even as she knelt in the bottom of the boat, which was beginning its perilous passage toward the shore, her eyes continued to be riveted upon his face, and she was saying to herself over and over:

"Oh! who is he, that boy? I must see him again if we both live. Can it be possible he had any connection with Paul's telegram? I have come far, but I would go over the distance a thousand times if only a great joy awaited me. Yes, I must see him surely again!"

From which it would appear that the friendly fortune that seemed to be attending the affairs of our young hero of late had again started work; and that even in gratifying his wild desire to serve as a life saver Darry had been advancing his own cause.

Now the lifeboat was headed for the shore, and sweeping in on a giant roller.

Great care had to be exercised lest the boat broach-to, and those in her be spilled out, when some must be drowned, for having taken so many aboard they lacked the buoyancy that had previously marked their progress.

Standing in his place the steersman carefully noted every little point, and high above the rush of the storm his voice rang out as he ordered the crew to cease rowing, or to pull hard.

It was well worth experiencing, and Darry was glad he had at last found a chance to go out with the crew.

Abner knew that at least one more trip would have to be made, in order to take off the crew of the steamer, and he was determined that if there should have arrived any substitute on the beach while they were away Darry must not be called upon to undertake the second voyage.

The strain was terrific for a mere stripling of his build, and only old seasoned veterans could stand under it.

There was no need of questioning the willingness of the lad to volunteer again; and if it seemed absolutely necessary Abner would give his consent, but he hoped circumstances might change and another hand be provided.

With the women and children they had several of the crew who had come along to relieve any oarsman who might give under the great strain; the more sent in this load the less remaining for the next, and among these Abner had picked upon a certain husky fellow who seemed able to do his part if called upon.

Now the shore was close by.

The fire burned brightly, fed by Paul, and the steersman could see several other men at the water's edge, proving that they had crossed the sound in some sort of staunch craft, or had come down from above, knowing the wreck was close to the life-saving station.

At last the boat mounted the last billow on which she was to continue her voyage to the beach.

The crew pulled heartily to keep her perched high on its foamy crest, and in this fashion they went rushing shoreward.

CHAPTER XXIV: THE AWAKENING

As the boat shot forward and her keel grated on the sand the crew were over the sides like a shot, seizing upon her in order to prevent the outgoing wave from carrying her along.

Then one by one the women and children were carried to the shore, and hurried to the shelter of the station, where a warm fire and something to drink in the way of coffee and tea would put new life in the shuddering mass.

The woman who had been so strangely agitated at sight of Darry seemed to be a lady of refinement, but she was almost perishing from the cold, and did not resist when they forced her to seek shelter.

Once she turned around and looked back to where Darry was busy; but when inside the house she swooned from exhaustion, to come to later and find Paul Singleton bending anxiously over her, with words of affection on his lips.

Meanwhile Darry was ready to again take his place with the rest, but Abner had been busy, and spoke to Mr. Frazer, who in turn engaged a stalwart fisherman to fill the vacancy caused by Tom's absence.

Although disappointed, Darry did not insist, for he knew the tax upon his young muscles had been severe, and if he failed it might throw the whole crew out of balance.

So he saw them set out again, with his heart in his eyes.

When they had vanished from view he walked nervously up and down the beach for a short time; then noticing the presence of a moving light not more than half a mile down the shore he remembered what he had heard Mr. Frazer say about the wreckers being abroad, looking for anything of value they could lay hands on.

Usually these men make their living by gathering up whatever may be cast on the beach after a vessel has gone to pieces, and thus far their calling is legitimate, but as a rule they are a bad class, and at times, when fortune frowns upon their efforts, many of their kind resort to desperate means for accumulating riches, even robbing the dead, and it was hinted in connection with Jim Dilks' crowd, going still further.

When a vessel is in danger of going to pieces, the passengers usually load themselves with what valuables they may possess in the hope of saving these in case they reach the shore in safety; so that these ghouls frequently find a little fortune upon the persons of the drowned travelers.

Darry had heard the crew of the lifeboat talking about these wreckers so frequently that he was more than curious with regard to them, and as he saw the lantern moving to and fro along the water's edge, now approaching and again retreating, he felt a sudden desire to look upon their methods of work. It was not a wise move on his part at all, for such men are as a rule desperate characters, and resent being spied upon, since such action savors too much of the law and justice in their eyes; but Darry was only a venturesome boy, who somehow never knew the meaning of the word fear, and a little saunter along the beach would pass away some of the time until the boat came in again.

So he started off, telling no one of his intention, though one man noticed him walk away, which fact proved fortunate in the end.

As he drew nearer the moving light he saw that, as he had suspected, it was a lantern held in the hand of a big man who was passing along as close to the edge of the water as he could, and surveying with the eye of a hawk each incoming billow, as though he expected to discover a floating form that must be snatched away ere it were carried out again.

But it was no errand of mercy that caused this human vulture to keep up his unceasing vigil; for should the body of a luckless passenger come ashore his first act would be to rifle the pockets rather than attempt to restore life.

Darry caught a glimpse of several other figures beyond, but their lanterns had evidently given out, so they were trusting to their eyes alone for seeing in the dark.

He had never as yet met big Jim Dilks, but something told him that this man was now before him, and he wondered if the son might not also be one of the other prowlers beyond, since he evidently possessed the same kind of savage instincts that characterized his father.

Darry had come as close as he deemed prudent when he saw the man start forward with a sudden swoop, and seizing some object from the inflowing wave drag it up on the shore.

There was no outcry to call the attention of others, for evidently this was a game of "every man for himself," though possibly a division of spoils might be made later on.

Horrified, Darry pressed closer, for he fancied he had seen a feeble movement on the part of the figure drawn from the waves—doubtless alone and unassisted the swimmer could never have crawled out on the beach, but now that he was beyond reach of the waves, would the man who had snatched him ashore do the slightest thing to keep the spark of life from going out entirely?

He saw Jim Dilks bend eagerly down.

Closer still Darry pressed, unconscious in his eagerness to see that he was placing his own life in danger.

The man who would not hesitate to rob the dead might go even further in order to conceal his crime.

He saw Jiw Dilks hurriedly search through the pockets of the figure, transfer a number of articles to his own person, and then with a growl lift the body in his arms, giving it a toss that once more sent it afloat.

The terrible nature of this act brought out a half-stifled cry from the watching boy, and the wrecker, startled, wheeled to see him there.

He darted upon him like a wolf, and ere Darry could lift a hand to save himself he was struck a severe blow on the head.

After that he knew nothing more.

When he opened his eyes later he found himself in the life-saving station, and for a minute or so wondered what had happened, for as he started to rise there was a severe pain in his head, and he sank back with a sigh.

Then it all seemed to pass before him.

Again he could see the savage face of big Jim, as he turned like a sheep-killing dog caught in the act, and once more Darry shivered with the terrible thought that life had not wholly departed from the wretched passenger from the ill-fated steamer at the time the wrecker tossed him back into the merciless sea.

Who had found him, and brought him here, when evidently the lawless man had intended that he should share the fate of the doomed passenger, and thus forever have his lips sealed?

Someone must have heard him sigh, for there was a movement close by, and his eyes took in the eager face of Paul Singleton.

"Bully for you, Darry! We were getting mighty anxious about you, but I can see you're all right now. It has been hard to keep Abner at his duty watching the shore. Every little while he appears at the door to ask if you have recovered your senses yet. Why, he couldn't be more fond of you if you were his own Joe," said Paul, running his hand tenderly over the boy's forehead.

"I don't understand how I got here," declared Darry; "the last thing I remember was being struck by the fist of that brute, big Jim Dilks. He had just robbed a passenger from the wreck. I saw him pull the body out of the water, clean out the pockets, and then throw the poor fellow back again. And, Mr. Singleton, it's a terrible thing to say, but I'm most sure there was life still in the body of the man he robbed when he tossed him back!"

"The scoundrel, I wouldn't put it past him a particle. And that isn't the first time he and his gang have done the same thing either. But their time has come, Darry. Even now I chance to know that the government has sent agents down here to make arrests, urged on by the women of Ashley, and before another day rolls around all of those rascals will be in the toils. You may be called on to give evidence against Dilks. But please forget all about this gruesome matter just now, my dear boy. There is something else of a vastly different nature that awaits you—some delightful intelligence, in fact."

Paul paused to let the half-dazed lad drink in the meaning of his words.

"Oh! Mr. Singleton!" he began.

"No, from this hour let it be Paul—Cousin Paul, in truth. You know, I said I wanted you to look upon me as an elder brother, but now it seems that we are actually related, and that I am your full-fledged cousin."

"My cousin! Oh! what can you mean?" gasped the bewildered Darry.

"I'll tell you without beating around the bush, then. You are no longer the poor homeless waif you used to believe yourself."

"No, that is true, thanks to dear old Abner and Nancy," murmured Darry, loyal to his good friends in this hour.

"But there is someone who has a better claim upon your affection than either Abner or Nancy, kind-hearted though they undoubtedly are. It is your own mother, Darry!" exclaimed the young man, leaning over closer as he said that word of magic.

"Mother! My mother! How sweet that sounds! But tell me how can this be? Who am I, and where is she? How did you find it out, and, oh! Paul, are you sure, quite sure? A disappointment after this would be hard to bear."

"Have no fears, Darry, there is no longer the slightest shadow of a doubt. The minute my aunt set her eyes on that crescent-shaped mark on your arm she knew beyond all question that Heaven had granted her prayers of years, and in this marvelous way restored her only child to her again. She saw you leap overboard to save that little child, and she recognized in your face the look she remembered so well as marking the countenance of her husband, now long since dead. She says you are his living picture as a boy."

"I remember some lady seizing hold of my arm after they dragged me aboard the lifeboat, but at the time I believed it must be the mother of the child, and I was anxious to get back to my place, for the boat might upset with one oar missing. And that was—my mother?"

How softly, how tenderly, he spoke the word, as though it might be something he had only dared dream about, and had difficulty in realizing now that he could claim what nearly all other boys had, a parent.

"Yes, that was my dear Aunt Elizabeth. I wired her away down in South America, where she was visiting cousins, and it has taken her quite a while to get here. She had to change steamers twice, and meant to come back here from New York by rail, when a strange freak of fortune sent that vessel upon the reef, and placed you in the lifeboat that went to the rescue. After this I shall stand in awe of the mysterious workings of Providence, since this beats anything I ever heard of. I could see something familiar in your looks, and after hearing your story sent for her on a chance. That was why I dared not tell you any more than I did. If I had only known about the history of that scar on your arm I would have been positive. She asked me immediately about it, and when I told her it was surely there she fainted again."

"My mother! how strange it seems. Go on please, Paul," murmured the boy, reaching out and possessing himself of the other's hand, as though its touch gave him assurance that this was not one of his tantalizing dreams.

"I went in search of you, and one of the men told me he had seen you walking down the beach, as though attracted by the light which he believed was a lantern carried by a wrecker, perhaps the feared Jim Dilks. I engaged him to accompany me, and securing a lantern we hurried along. And Darry, we found you just in time, for the sea was carrying you out. I believe that wretch must have cast you into the water just as he did the body of the passenger."

"Then I owe my life to you—Cousin Paul?"

"If so it only squares accounts, for I guess I'd have gone under out there on the sound only for your coming in time. But Darry, do you think you feel strong enough to see your mother? I forced her to lie down in the little room beyond, but she cannot sleep from the excitement."

"Yes, oh! yes. Please bring her. I shall be a long time understanding it all, and trying to realize that I am truly awake. To think that I really have a mother!"

Darry drew a long breath, and followed Paul with eager eyes as he went through the doorway into the other room.

It was dawn now.

In more senses than one the day had come to Darry.

He heard low voices, and then someone came through the door, someone whose eyes were fastened hungrily upon his face.

Darry struggled to sit up, and was just in time to feel a pair of arms around his neck and have his poor aching head drawn lovingly upon the bosom of the mother whom he had not known since infancy.

CHAPTER XXV: CONCLUSION

Later on, in fragments, Darry learned the whole story. It was all very wonderful, and yet simple enough.

The old man whom he remembered so well, and who had told him to call him uncle, was in reality a brother of his mother.

He had quarreled with his sister Elizabeth's husband, after abusing his kindness, and to cancel what he called a debt, had actually stolen the only child of the man he had wronged and hated.

An old story, yet happening just as frequently in these modern days as in times of old, for men have the same passions, and there is nothing new under the sun.

Everything that money could do was done to find the man and the little boy he had kidnapped, but he proved too cunning for them all, and although several times traces were found of his being at some foreign city, when a hunt was made he had again vanished.

So the years came and went, and the child's mother was left a widow.

Hope never deserted her heart, though it must have grown fainter as time passed on, and all traces of the wicked child-stealer seemed swallowed up in mystery.

Paul had known of her great trouble, and it was the remarkable resemblance of Darry to a picture he had seen of his uncle Rudolph as a boy that first startled him.

Then came the story about the waif, and this gave him strong hopes that by the wonderful favor of Providence he had been enabled to come across the long-lost boy, his own cousin.

Their happiness was subdued, for there had been lives lost in the storm, a number of passengers and crew having been swept from the deck of the steamer by the giant waves before the coming of the life savers.

As the storm subsided by noon, our little party, increased by Abner's presence, was enabled to cross the still rough sound in the staunch motor-boat of Paul, and to Nancy's amazement appeared at her humble little home.

She heard the story of Darry's great good fortune with mingled emotions, for while she could not but rejoice with him in that he had found a mother, still, in a way, it seemed to the poor woman as though she had been bereaved a second time, for she was beginning to love the boy who had come into her life to take the place of Joe.

Still, the future appeared so rosy that even Nancy could not but feel the uplift, and her face beamed with the general joy as she bustled around and strove to prepare a supper for her guests.

In the village they had heard news.

Jim Dilks and several of his cronies were in the hands of the United States authorities, having been arrested on serious charges.

Later on they were convicted of using false beacons in order to lure vessels on the reefs for wicked purposes, and of robbing the dead cast up on the shore.

A more serious charge could not be proven, though few doubted their innocence.

Darry, or as he was compelled to call himself now, Adrian Singleton, being summoned to give evidence, helped to send the big wrecker to his well-earned solitude by telling what he had seen on the night of the last storm, and as some jewelry was found in his possession, which was identified by the wife of a passenger who lost his life, and whose body was washed up on the beach later on, there was no difficulty in securing his conviction.

As for his profligate son, he was not long in following the elder Dilks to confinement, being caught in some crime that partook of the nature of robbery, and was sent to a reformatory, where it is to be hoped he may learn a lesson calculated to make him a better man when he comes forth.

Since these happenings took place only a few years back, young Jim is still in confinement; his boon companions Sim Clark and Bowser vanished from Ashley and doubtless sought congenial surroundings in Wilmington, where they could pursue their destiny along evil lines until the long arm of the law reached out and brought them to book.

True to his word, Paul saw to it that Abner Peake was placed in charge of the big farm he owned, not a great distance away from Ashley, and here the former life saver and his family have every comfort their simple hearts could wish for, so that they count it the luckiest day of their lives when the cabin boy of the lost brigantine, Falcon, was washed up on the beach out by the life-saving station.

About once a year Abner visits his old chums out on the beach, spending a couple of days in their company and reviving old times, but on such occasions they often see him sitting by himself under the shelter of some old remnant of a former wreck, his calm blue eyes fixed in an absent-minded fashion upon the distant level horizon of Old Ocean, and at such times no one ventures to disturb him, for well they know that he is holding silent communion with the spirit of poor little Joe, who went out with the tide, and was seen no more.

Somewhere upon that broad, lonely ocean his little form has found a resting place, and so long as he lives must Abner drop a tear in his memory whenever he sets eyes upon his watery shroud.

But the Peakes are happy, and the twins are growing up to be buxom children.

There is another little laughing Peake now, a boy at that, and at last accounts Darry—it is hard to call him by any other name—heard that he is destined to be christened Joseph Darry Peake.

After all, Paul and Darry did have a chance to spend some part of the winter cruising together on the sound, although our hero later on decided that he must start in to make himself worthy of the position which was from this time to be his lot, and enrolled at an academy where his fond mother could be near him, and have a home in which he might find some of the happiness that fate had cheated him out of for so long.

No one who knows the youth doubts that he has a promising future before him, and many prophesy that he will eventually make a more famous lawyer than his father was before him.

Often Darry loves, when by himself, to look back to the days that are no more, and at such times he thinks with gratitude of the friends whom a kindly Providence raised up for him in his time of need.

Among these he never fails to include Captain Harley, the skipper of the Falcon, whose widow Darry had communicated with while he was still under the roof of the life saver's home, and whom he later on met personally, as she came on to hear all he could tell about her lost husband.

And the brave life savers on that desolate Carolina beach have not been forgotten by the grateful mother of the boy they had adopted, for during each winter there always comes a huge box filled with such warm clothing as men in their arduous and dangerous profession greatly need.

At Christmas holidays Darry, Paul and Mrs. Singleton make it a point to spend a week at Ashley, during which time they live again the stirring scenes of the past, and find much cause for gratitude because of the wonderful favors that were showered upon them in that locality.

THE END

Made in the USA
Monee, IL
03 October 2023